The Dog Under The Bed

DJ Cowdall

This is a work of fiction. Any names or characters, businesses or places, events or incidents, are fictitious. Any resemblance to actual persons, living or dead, or actual events is purely coincidental.

http://www.davidcowdall.com

https://twitter.com/djcowdall

https://www.facebook.com/DJCowdall

https://www.instagram.com/djcowdall

ISBN-10: 1983702935

Other Works By DJ Cowdall

Novels

The Dog That Wouldn't Sit

Missing

The Dog Under The Bed 2: Arthur On The Streets

The Dog Under The Bed 3: What Happened Next

Two Dogs In Africa

Hypnofear

I Was A Teenage Necromancer: Book 1

I Was A Teenage Necromancer: Book 2: Supernature

The Magic Christmas Tree

The Kids of Pirate Island

53%

Short Stories

Inferno

Kites

Sacrifice

A Breath of Magic

Available from all good booksellers

ACKNOWLEDGMENTS

Cover Art by Olivia
Pro Design

For Bet

CHAPTER ONE

I want to tell you a story, but it's not a fantasy story, of dragons or myths, but about a dog, a very special dog. This one can't fly, he can't do magic tricks, and he can't talk. So what makes him so special, well, you see he has a crafty way about him, one that throughout his life he has used to make sure he is warm, relatively well fed and lucky in all manner of ways.

Now I can't tell you every single thing that happened to him, but I can tell you of one particular incident, that I witnessed firsthand. Let me begin, as is best in these kinds of things, at the beginning.

OK, maybe in the middle: he ate an apple!

No, seriously though, I'll go back to the very beginning, as much as I understand it.

It was late autumn, and the nights were closing in fast. Clocks went back one hour early on a Sunday morning, and by then we knew it was just going to get colder. Going for walks when all the leaves have turned brown and fallen from the trees is all very well, and much fun, but when you're stuck outside in it, it's no fun at all.

Now, the dog in question, his name is Arthur. Don't ask me why he was called Arthur, because I don't know, and I suspect when he got that name, those who gave it to him had no clue either.

Now Arthur was an interesting little chap, medium sized, brown fur, black muzzle, and he was no pedigree. He had these large white whiskers that stuck out, and if you touched them, or anything did, he would shy away. Same with his paws, you could rub his back all day long and he would just love you in spades for it, but touch his paws and he would pull them away. Such a fun and loving dog, well you would never imagine any like that would be an unwanted stray, but he was, and he knew it.

Home to Arthur was where dogs went, and all too often never came out from again, so he made sure that his home was the roads and anywhere that the dog catcher wouldn't find him.

How old was he? Who knows, he seemed ageless, boundless energy, and just when it took his pleasure he would suddenly sprint around acting the fool. Woe betide any cardboard box that got in his way, it would feel his teeth on its corners and would be quick to join in the frenetic fun, bouncing all over like a dog who wanted to be a clown.

Another thing about Arthur, well he was always hungry, I mean if he saw food you would think he was hypnotized, his gaze staring at it, he wouldn't even blink! His eyes would follow any piece of food, this way and that, like there was an invisible piece of string attached between it and his head, and when you twisted it this way and that, his eyes and head followed it exactly.

The year in question, as much as it was late autumn, it was a very wet time. I mean it rained so much you would think we all needed to buy a boat and get to safety. Of course, it wasn't really that bad, but anyone or any dog outside in that certainly wouldn't enjoy it. Big coats and wellington boots don't go well on a dog, he keeps falling over.

So that time Arthur knew he needed somewhere to get warm. He just so happened to be wandering down the streets, minding his own business, stopping to cock his leg every now and then so he could pretend he had something left to leave his mark, when a huge gust of wind came rushing in, directly in his direction. Piles of leaves and bits of paper and all sorts rushed around him like a whirlwind, and he looked like Toto, about to fly off to the land of Oz.

Arthur wasn't prone to panicking, but he knew he often had a few more weeks to find somewhere decent to rest up for the worst of the weather, and this little flash was a bit of a shock to him. Normally Arthur would find an old abandoned warehouse, or someplace like it where he could wait it out, find an easy stash of food and just chill, while all the other dogs sat out in the rain like the boneheads he thought they were.

Now, don't take it that Arthur was a bad dog, or had a poor attitude towards other dogs, because he didn't. He was as loving and compassionate as any dog can be. It was just that he had some common sense, and for anyone who had known dogs, well you will know dogs aren't best suited for doing the sensible thing. Arthur was.

Now Warrington was no longer the place to find run-down buildings or warehouses, no empty shops or factories he could sneak into. Dog catchers were all around, and nobody wanted to take in street smart mangy mutts, if they weren't gorgeous little creatures with puppy dog eyes. He was fine with that, just common sense, his watchword for survival.

Arthur was walking up Battersby Lane, passing under the railway bridge, cars flying past too fast as they always do on that stretch, just as this mini storm hit, almost sending him flying. It was a crazy moment, but just the shock he needed to get himself into gear. He certainly didn't want to see his big ears flapping all over and a chill wind sending his dirty coat into a spin, let alone heavy rain giving him the one thing he disliked above all: a bath!

It was an emergency, and he went full runaway chicken mode, first trying to cross the road, before car horns warned him away, then into a local garden, just as the wind slammed a gate on him, right up to old Mrs. Hannigan as she was walking back from Sainsbury's with her shopping. Poor Mrs. Hannigan couldn't drive and didn't have anyone to do it for her, so every other day back and forth with her goods, and then Arthur comes storming up in full panic mode, avoiding her but knocking both her shopping bags out of her hands, spilling across the path.

"Out of the way, you mangy mutt!" Mrs. Hannigan called out to him, and Arthur looked like a football being knocked this way and that. He didn't know which way to turn. Everywhere he looked there were cars, old ladies, leaves, and debris chasing him everywhere.

Our poor little canine friend was terrified, eyes wide open and mouth flapping around as if he were tumbling uncontrollably down a hill. He sprinted as fast as his little legs would take him, this way and that, towards the road, then back, until he found a small gap in a low fence and broke through towards some high rise, three-story houses. All along were perfect gardens, dying flowers, bushes and nothing out of place. Arthur sprinted as if he were a horse in a race, past Mister Bloomsberry's shorn roses, across Mister Dandridge's lawn, down the gap between two hugely tall houses and into the back garden, under a gap in the fence, broken when young Timothy ran his bicycle into it. Out into another garden, scurrying around, chased by the nonexistent wind and a massive pile of leaves that weren't really there, until he came across a door, an open door, into a dark place that looked far more safe than anything else that had presented itself to him.

Arthur may have been afraid of his own shadow, often jumping when he looked behind himself in the sunshine to see something dark and foreboding beside him, but he was never short of being crafty.

That, dear reader, is where this unusual tale truly begins, because when an opportunity such as this presented itself to Arthur, he would never turn it down. The way was clear, but still he was just smart enough to ensure he wouldn't do anything rash. Besides, Arthur was never a great fan of running.

He stopped, hunching down, looking like he was going to pounce any moment, his senses alive, as much as he could manage, being such a sleepy type. The doorway ahead looked dark, but it was open, safe and inviting. Should he take a chance, or should he slink away and hide behind a shed?

Just as he was about to make his choice, the faint aroma of something wonderful caught his nose, tugging at it like a fishing rod to a kipper. It was something he recognized, a fine sweet smell, cooked chicken. It was like a red flag to a bull, a neon sign calling his name, *come on in, enjoy, you're welcome*.

Arthur edged forward, one paw slowly in front of the other, all sense out of the window now as he breathed in the gorgeous smells. He drew up to the door, slowly peered inside, seeing the long narrow hallway, nobody there, seeing a door ahead and another to the side. He looked left, then right, all the while trembling slightly, his dog senses working overdrive, a royal battle between the love of food and the fear of being caught. He put his left paw inside, crouching still, looking slowly around, feeling the cold hard floor against his worn pads. It was a strange sensation, so long since he had been in any place that had people, but he just couldn't resist.

A long narrow hall surrounded by doors stood before him, with an unusually warm gust of wind coming from above. It was a plain place to see, nothing so welcoming, but the warm air from the flight of stairs leading up was too much to bear, and so feeling intrepid he headed up, slowly, watching all the time, looking right up and listening intently.

At the top Arthur straightened up a little, lifting his head to see another long hallway, doors either side and another flight of stairs leading up, as if the house went on forever. At the end of the hall was the kitchen, door open, warmth and light spilling out like a dream come true for a cold, hungry little dog.

"Can I have another piece?" someone asked. Arthur froze, as if someone had hit him with a freeze ray and he was glued to the spot. His little heart beat so fast and loud he thought it might pop out of his chest at any moment. Should he stay, should he run?

On a table in the room ahead appeared to be a banquet, from a glorious place, somewhere that even he might enjoy being, no matter what others thought. Arthur wondered, what would they make of him? Would they really welcome a little brown dog, one with a habit of smelling bad and licking himself so loud he sounded like a bath draining? Probably not.

So it was back outside, carry on, find something gross to eat, and hope the weather didn't turn too bad. With a sad look on his face, Arthur turned and looked down the darkened stairs, to see the heavens truly open and a downpour of the heaviest rain he could ever imagine.

"Can I have a drink?" a voice asked.

"Sure," said Dad. "Go get yourself one," he says.

"Awww, Dad," a young voice cries, sounding as if they are approaching.

Panic, rain, thunder, snow, hail, well, not all of them, but to a small dog, it can easily seem so. Arthur went into full-on panic mode again, looking all around as if a loud and heavy voice would scream at him, that he would be chased and so afraid again. He lost sight of where he should be going, turning quickly and heading up more stairs, not outside to the rain, but to somewhere even warmer, quieter.

"I need the toilet," another voice called, a different one, and so Arthur felt surrounded. He leaped ahead, up to the top, then down along a hall, no idea where he was going, leaping and bounding along until he saw a safe space, a low hung long thing, with darkness underneath, to which he dived in, sliding in, without a clue what was to come.

Arthur turned a little, as he curled his body up, tail between his legs, eyes wide open, wondering how long before the strangers come for him, before the room filled with those people, and off he went. Arthur waited, and waited, but nobody came.

It was dark there, but warm, and there was lots under there, little of which he could see. It was quiet, and perhaps safe, for now. So he hid, slinking back into the dark corner, smooth wall behind him, and allowed himself to drift off, eyes closing, into beautiful sleep.

Arthur dozed and dreamed, under the bed. His adventure had begun.

CHAPTER TWO

"Muuuuum, I can't find my pajama top!" a voice hollered. Arthur jumped with such surprise, as he lifted to see what was going on, he cracked his head on the underside of the bed. Thankfully it was between the wooden slats, so didn't hurt much. He struggled to yawn, in between trying to open his sleepy eyes and at the same time see and hear what was going on. It felt like work, and he so disliked anything that involved work.

'Muuuuuum!" the voice screamed again. Arthur's ears dropped, as the terrible noise closed in on him.

"Billy, it's probably under your bed," another voice answered, sounding older. Arthur couldn't speak human, so he had no idea what they were saying, but from a life on the streets, his instincts were good, and he could just tell something was going to happen.

A shape dropped down beside the edge of the place he hid in, as an arm began reaching out in his direction. It looked like a giant octopus, slithering along, moving this way and that trying to catch a fish. He slunk back further into the darkness, pushing aside smelly clothes, a plate and a range of small plastic soldiers, none of which were a problem.

A hard wall tapped at Arthur's bottom, reminding him it was there, and that now he was in a corner, no matter how dark, there was no other place to go.

Arthur began to shake, worried that all was lost. The little boy would spot him, jump up and run out shouting for help, and then the world would end.

Of course, it didn't, but it had before, and a lonely dog might be forgiven for thinking the worst. After all, so long being alone, he had forgotten what it was to be loved.

"Gottit!" the little boy shouted, dragging his arm out and standing quickly. All Arthur could see were a pair of feet, stood beside the bed, toes wriggling around, looking at him as if they knew his secret.

"Good, now go brush your teeth and come watch TV for a little while,'" the older voice said. The little boy ran.

It all went quiet, as little Arthur settled once again. It was still scary, but he felt a little warmer, had enjoyed his sleep, and now all he could think about was food, mostly chicken. He laid his hairy chin on the soft floor, allowing his eyes to adjust to the low light, looking out through the doorway, wondering where he had gotten himself. He didn't like being inside, but for there and then it was better than being battered by rain. Just as he was thinking that, a heavy gust of wind pressed a blast of rain to the window high above, reminding him of his good choice.

Arthur had a new choice, to remain where he was and hope it would work out, or have a look around. It was quiet again, but he knew it could change any moment. As he lifted his head, he looked at the dimming lights from outside, and wondered how he might even get out at all. As he looked, a sudden sensation caught his attention, one that came with a mixture of feelings and thoughts. He could certainly smell food, but with it a sweet sickly smell. He began sniffing, his black, wet, pointy nose taking in drops of air here and there, his head bobbing around, trying to find the source of it.

It may well have been too dark to see, but regardless, Arthur was experienced enough to know food when he smelled it, but more importantly toast, cold yes, dry yes, but still it was toast! The problem his nose was telling him, was that it was stuck underneath a particularly smelly sock, draped across the plate. The young boy had his good habits and his bad habits, and the good was leaving food on a plate under his bed, the bad leaving old clothes in the same place.

He had always assumed he was something of a beggar, and of course beggars can't be choosers, so he went for it. There was no easy way to do it, as he took a hold of the three-week-old sweaty sock in his mouth, lifting it away and dropping it as far away as he could get it without going out into the garden and burying it.

Then, it appeared before him, the shining spectacle of a feat. To us, it was nothing more than moldy bread, green here and there, covered in fluff, but to a hungry street dog, one that didn't smell much better than moldy bread, well it was worthy of a king. Arthur lunged at the toast, toyed with it a second, then swallowed it so quickly he was coughing up bread crumbs, before licking them back up again.

It was wonderful.

Creeping darkness edged over everything in the room, but it was far from scary. Instead, all Arthur could feel was warmth, which was precious. It was the first time in many moons that he had been able to lay anywhere settled, and not have to worry about passing strangers, animals bigger than he was, rain or cold winds. Even if the time it allowed prove to be only brief, at least he would be able to enjoy a moment of proper, decent rest.

Arthur decided he had time to kill and wanted something to do. He was never so foolish to believe he could go wandering in a strange house, without being seen, or smelled! However, he did know that he needed a wash. A wash that is, not a bath, not a shower, just a wash. The last time he had been given a bath was when some loud young men threw him in the canal, and he came out smelling worse. The last time he had a shower was every single time it rained and he was outside.

His wash consisted of licking himself, with his not so clean tongue, but it was the best there was, and he enjoyed it, especially if he licked himself in certain ways. His bottom wasn't the nicest, but needs must.

A light stomping noise interrupted him mid lick, as he lay there looking into the darkness, his mouth partially open, tongue stuck to his front paw, looking and listening for impending doom. The stomping grew louder until it sounded as if a herd of elephants was approaching. Arthur lifted his head, eyes wide, looking to see any signs of their moving towards him. All he could see were shadows.

A light flicked on outside the room as the stomping descended into hollering. The light flickered, then grew brighter until its rays spread across into the room. Arthur's eyes glowed like twin neons, signaling he was there and watching. He was sometimes a lucky dog, and this was one of those times. If the children had seen him, they would have screamed in terror at the thing under the bed, horrible eyes staring out at them, not realizing he was a cuddly if smelly dog.

Fearful of the noise, Arthur slunk back closer to the corner, hiding and making himself as small as he could. Another light flicked on in the room, making him jump. So much noise, so much going on, so bright and easy to see, but still, there were lots of things under the bed, toys, blankets, all sorts of mess, and plenty to hide behind.

"Can I have a story?" a young boy asked. He was standing on the edge of his bed, wearing Spider-man pajamas, bare feet, hopping around as if his feet were burning.

"Do you need the toilet?" someone asked, much older, a woman.

"No," the boy replied.

"Then why are you hopping around?" the woman asked again.

A brief moment of quiet as the boy stopped moving, then laughter. "Dunno," he said, giggling. The woman laughed with him.

Another pair of legs entered the room, only this time it was a young girl, wearing a nightie. Hers said Princess Abigail in big letters, and she, unlike her brother, didn't hop. Instead, she held onto a mobile phone.

"Mum, I need some credit," the girl asked.

"What happened to the last lot?" the woman asked. The girl turned and walked out, back off into another room.

"Well, get into bed then," the woman said, clearly talking to the boy. He jumped into his bed, making it sag and bounce, tapping Arthur on his head, as he tried to crawl ever further into the corner of his newfound home.

"But I want Teddy, where is Teddy?" the boy pleaded, continuing to bounce up and around in his bed, and so in turn on Arthur's head.

"You'll mess up your covers, be still will you?" the woman asked. Arthur could see she was wearing slippers, with white fur around the ankles. He thought how comfy they looked, and how much he would love to cuddle up to them, or even better, how much he would like to chew them to pieces and throw them all over the room.

"Teddy," the boy pleaded again.

"Well, where is he? Is he under your bed?" the woman asked. Now, obviously Arthur couldn't speak human, he could barely speak dog, so at that he had no idea what she was asking, but what frightened him the most was how she immediately began to bend over, one hand on the bed, and made to look underneath. Arthur lifted his head again from being crouched and hidden, looking like a rabbit in the headlights of an oncoming car. It was time to run because there was nowhere else to hide.

Arthur wasn't a fighter, he chose to cringe or run, whichever worked best. So far it had just about worked, a few scrapes, but nothing too bad, but now he was well and truly trapped, anything could happen.

Being such a timid little chap, he began to shake, afraid that he was in trouble.

"No, it's on the drawers over there," the little boy said. The woman stopped mid bend, waited a moment, then lifted up again, walking over to some drawers in the corner.

Arthur flapped his tail, unaware that he was doing so, and besides, even if he had not wanted his tail to flap there was nothing he could do about it, it had a life of its own. Sometimes when he was outside and he was laid eating a tasty morsel he had found he would stop and just look at his tail, as if flailed around like some snake that had suddenly appeared. If dogs could laugh, he surely often would have at the oddness of it.

No matter, it was soft and small, and not enough for anyone to notice. Arthur could have relaxed, but still, it was bright and noisy and the bed kept bouncing.

"Here you are, now time to go to sleep. Give me a kiss and say night-night," the woman insisted, polite and loving with it, but still firm in her own way. Arthur thought he liked her, just from how she sounded. She moved closer to the bed, leaned against it a little and kissed the boy.

"Night-night, Mummy," the boy said, still shuffling around.

The woman walked away, the light was flicked off and the door pulled to. The noisy commotion continued down the hall, but for now, peace settled on the little room. The bed continued to bounce and move around as the little boy quietly drifted away into sleep, and little Arthur, warm as he had ever been, snug in his little escape, surrounded by smelly socks and worn out comics, toys and plates, all sorts of junk, joined in. Together they slept like angels.

The bliss didn't last, as a minor rumbling sound provoked a response. At first, it was difficult to make out where it was coming from, and Arthur decided he was too comfy to move anyway, but he lay, eyes wide open trying to see in the darkness, wondering what the noise was.

The sound rumbled, then gurgled, then something moved near him. Panic was close to setting in, when the rumbling and gurgling noise, the feeling that was so close, became very apparent, in his stomach. He wasn't so much hungry as starving. In the house there were no dropped burgers, no bins with packs of chips, no cartons of cakes or dropped bits and pieces, food galore he could tuck into. He would have to be creative.

The rumbling in his tummy persisted, nagging at him, like a voice demanding he go get some food!

Slowly Arthur crawled from under the bed, edging forward like a soldier sneaking through the marshes, trying to find his destination. If Arthur had black paint around his eyes and a backpack he would truly have looked the military part.

He stood out from the bed, having slept so soundly he might well have been battery operated and switched off. He stretched, so slowly, pulling on all his limbs until his chin stuck out into the air. He thought about shaking, one of his favorite pastimes, but was wary of waking the little boy up, and so would wait. He could get somewhere that no one else was and have the greatest stretch and shake of all time.

The next stage, after ensuring no one was around, was to sniff. His nose was black, with white whiskers around his muzzle, something which people often thought made him look cute; not cute enough to be taken in, sadly for him.

Slowly he walked across the room, towards the door, until his gaze met opening. He looked through, seeing darkness on the other side. It was a long hallway, something he had barely noticed when he was running to and fro in such a panic. He leaned out, noticing a door stood at the end, partly opened, with a small night light peeking through, likely the little girl's room. Across from him stood two more doors, one closed, the other wide open. In the open one were shiny tiles and all white, looking like the kind of place he had seen often, where people went to cock their legs to do a wee, only sometimes they would sit down and do it. Arthur had once tried to copy doing his business in this manner, only he had ended up with a sticky bum and regretted it for days, until rain washed it off. No way was he going to lick that off!

The sound of dripping water from the room opposite made him think to get a drink, as there was a bowl in there which appeared specifically for dogs to drink from, at least as long as the lid wasn't down. His tummy rumbled some more, as if it had a voice that shouted to him, not water, food! It was good, he could have both, food first, then water. To his left were the stairs he had come up on, and all around on the floor was soft, thick carpet. As he walked towards the stairs he couldn't help but notice how fine it felt underneath his paws, each step like walking on soft leaves on a summer day. He was lucky.

Sadly, Arthur was never often a lucky dog, and that night his luck was no better. As he got to the end of the hall, standing on the edge of the steep stairs, looking down, a door loudly clicked, the hall light flicked on, bright lights illuminated him stood right there, and a man walked out, dressed in light blue pajamas with a picture of a moose on the back.

All was lost, Arthur's ears shot up, any last remnants of tiredness disappeared, his senses come alive. Now he would need to run again. His tummy could rumble all it wanted, he wouldn't be eating after all.

The man staggered out into the hallway, arms outstretched fumbling along the wall. Arthur was frozen to the spot, unable to find the release to just run or hide. He just stood, watching, waiting for the loud noise as the man finally saw him and shouted, like an elephant roaring, before rampaging towards him to gobble him up.

The man pushed his head back, opened his mouth wide, but instead of a shout, he did what all good dogs, and apparently humans do, he yawned, so loud and long Arthur couldn't resist joining in. Both man and dog stood, yawning wide, enjoying every last moment of it, before settling.

Then, back to it, ready for fight or flight. The man stumbled along, feet barely spaced apart, shuffling across the oh-so-soft carpet, heading directly for Arthur, without even having the decency to look at him.

Arthur stood like a statue, bewildered by it all. As he watched, the man continuing his trek, before turning into the room with the shiny tiles and flowing water bowls, and closed the door. It was as if the little dog was invisible, that when he stood still no one could see him, he could come and go at will.

Of course, Arthur wasn't daft enough to believe that, he knew better from experience, if they didn't see him, someone would certainly smell him! Still, it had been amazing, and gave him great courage. Before anyone else could come out, someone who actually walked around with their eyes open, Arthur did the best thing and ran down the stairs. He knew he could have gone back into the bedroom, hidden under the bed, but then his stomach would moan about it and he couldn't have that.

The stairs were steep, and as he went down the light from above diminished. He was thankful for some darkness that he might hide better, but still, it was difficult. As he saw the flat ground ahead he felt comforted, safe again that he was...

As he congratulated himself on doing so well, being too full of himself, he tripped, rolling over, head over heels, tumbling down like a giant fur-ball, tail flapping around as he twisted this way and that trying to stand up as the stairs threw him only one way. As he crashed into the next hallway he rolled and gently hit the corner wall beyond, before coming to a full stop, upside down, tail tickling his face, legs up in the air. He looked a sight, if anyone had seen him they would have thought only one thing: what on earth was he doing?

No matter. No one had noticed. The light above flicked off, shuffling carpet sounds suggested the adult had gone the right way, and a door clicking confirmed he had gone back to bed.

Arthur stood up, shook gently and looked around. He was tired and fancied another few hours of sleep, but for now, his nose would need to do its job. He looked around, realizing he still wasn't at the place where he came in. The house he had gone into was huge, as big as anything he had ever seen, and all of it warm and loving. At least it was for adults.

Ahead were a number of other doors, all of them slightly open. He would walk through each one and see what was what, like an intrepid explorer wandering colorful wasteland in search of treasure.

The door at the end of the hall was completely open, and the most inviting. It was lit up from outside by moonlight, and he could see enough to recognize it was a place where food was stored. He paced ahead, noticing the still soft carpet, albeit a different color. As he entered the room the floor changed to tiles, making it obvious how large the entire place was. To one corner were a table and chairs, with counters and worktops opposite. Along them were various items that Arthur had seen before but didn't much understand. There was a large white thing, with double doors. He had seen that before too, but knew it was difficult to open, and another thing next to it which had pans and pots on.

He walked slowly in, before standing directly before the thing with pots and pans, then raised his head up to sniff again. There were no scents, nothing, it was all just too spic and span, clean as a polished button.

His tummy called out again, sounding like a drain emptying out. Something had to give, even it if meant him chewing his way into a place where food lay. As his need grew, his super-sensitive nose caught wind of something nice, something he knew would lead to just the treasure he needed. It was coming from the far end, the opposite corner to the table and chairs, a tall, thin object, round and smooth. He knew this too, had seen what adults did with them, stuffing all those goodies in, things that they no longer wanted, but he would glory in.

The tall round thing was too high for him to get into, and there was nothing beside it to climb on to reach down from. No matter, he wasn't going to give up that easily. Arthur jumped at it, trying to put his front paws on top. He rested a moment, stretching as much as he could, even his tail pointing to the ground as if it could make him taller. The bin shifted a little as his head bobbed and shifted around, nose sniffing like a vacuum cleaner seeking out yummy grub.

Too bad, a lid sat on top, small and round, blocking his access. Still, he needed it, had to have it. Just as he leaned in, as his wet nose toyed with the lid, the bin could take no more, at first slowly leaning a little, before towering over, and dropping, like a metal brick. It crashed to the floor, sending Arthur rolling around again. The lid flipped off, sending pieces of food and small bags all over the floor. It was like a clown act at a circus, with his big nose and wagging tail he could entertain anyone looking on. Lucky for him no one was.

Arthur jumped up at the loud bang, frightened by something he did himself, then wondering how long before someone would come charging in. He had no time, but a great need, would he hide? Would he eat? What was there? It was all too much for him and all the while his stomach was telling him its need was greater than anything else.

Food overrode common sense and Arthur just got back to dealing with it. He pawed at small white tied bags, dragging them out across the floor, then used his teeth to pull them apart. Finally, bits of food spilled across the floor. Some cheesy pizza, some rice, even a meatball, it was heaven, he had struck gold and was lapping it up. If he could he would have picked it up and carried it all back to his bed, but he was so hungry it wasn't an option. Food in normal life for him was something he got in scraps, here and there.

The biggest meal he had had up until that point had been a full hamburger, one that had been accidentally dropped by a young girl on a bike. He had felt guilty about it, even wondered if he should go and tell her she had dropped it, but didn't, mainly because he couldn't talk, so instead grabbed a hold of it and ran away. Anyone seeing him would have thought what a naughty little dog, but hey, at least he thought about being nice.

Besides, if he had taken it back to her she might not have liked the fact it had been in his mouth. Humans were funny like that, his mouth was perfectly clean. Sort of.

The meatball was extremely tasty, he loved meat, but the pizza was best, so much so that by the time he had finished it his muzzle was covered in tomato sauce. He tried licking it off, but even though his tongue was so big it looked like a necktie, he still couldn't get at it all. No matter, he could save that for later.

Arthur stopped a moment to survey his conquest, the wrappers, papers, and boxes all over, before burping long and loud. It had been a feast, not quite perfect because there had been no pudding, none of his favorite dropped to the floor ice cream, but still, as he always said, beggars can't be choosers, and he had been spoiled.

It was back to bed time. The early break of the light of dawn was creeping up over the windows, and he knew once that was in full flow humans would rise up and take over once again.

This time he handled the stairs better, no more rolling around as if he were a football, he sprang up, feeling his full and heavy stomach lurching around inside him. One step, three steps and up he went, to the landing. Still, he was cautious, didn't want to spoil a lovely night, so he stopped at the edge of the stairs, looking around. Nobody home. First door on the right, the one he knew was safe.

He slowly crept in, nudged the door a little wider, walked gently in, spotted his favorite darkened hiding place and trudged towards it. As he got halfway across the floor, a chirping sound interrupted him mid-walk. He stopped, glued to the ground, wondering what it was. He looked up to the window, wondering if it were birdsong. No, it wasn't that. Next, he looked to his right, no, nothing there but a wall with a poster on it of a man in funny colors and a cape. Then he looked slowly round to his right, not moving forward or back at all. Then, he saw it, the bed covers removed, the little boy, he was sat on the floor, holding a toy soldier. He was lost in thought, making sounds to match his imagination.

Arthur stared at him, watching and listening to the little boy as he enjoyed himself. He was sat, surrounded by toys, appearing as happy as the day he was born. Daylight had continued its long creep into the house, and was now enough that anything could be seen, including a little dog slinking along.

There had never been so many difficult decisions to make in all of his little life until now, and each one either brought with it loud shouting, chasing and panic, or food and sleep in short comfort.

The chirping sound had, of course, come from the boy, not birds outside as he had thought. It was both a worry and a blessing, a reminder that he was indeed indoors, in the warmth, somewhere nice.

With nothing to lose, Arthur walked as slowly as he could, much like the snail he had once seen walk past him as he lay in a storm drain in summer. Then he had been intrigued by it, how slow it was, but upset the poor thing by pawing it, then playing with it until it rolled off and disappeared into some bushes Arthur had laid there wondering if snails always rolled, unaware that it had only done so because of him.

Carefully he went, not wishing to be discovered, but also because he didn't want to spoil the little boy's dreams, envious of being so happy, able to sit and allow his mind to wander off to something amazing. Such was the life of a child.

The bed almost seemed to come to him, as he lowered his back and crawled ever so carefully underneath it once again. It felt welcoming, like he had a proper home for the first time in his life. It wasn't perfect, but as long as no one knew about it, he would feel safe.

Finally, he was in, curled up back in the corner, the walls behind him, hidden in the secret place only he knew about.

The moment he felt settled the door pushed open hard, knocking the boy in the back. A young girl walked in, the same mobile phone in her hand.

"Come on Billy, get up!" she called smartly. She looked skyward, as if she were an angel singing to the clouds, telling them it was morning.

"Ouch," the little boy said, rubbing his back.

The girl looked down, seeing her brother sat with his toys.

"Can I play?" she asked, not waiting for an answer. She sat, pocketing her phone. She watched on, sat next to a dark green colored soldier, on Billy's bedroom battlefield.

"Hey, the general said no, you cannot play here, only boys are allowed," the boy said, picking up the girl's phone, throwing it out of the room. He made a whizzing noise as it flew, as if it were a missile being fired.

"Mum, Billy just threw my phone," the girl shouted. Arthur's ears dropped, fearful of all the commotion. He never liked shouting, it was all just a little too much for a peace-loving dog like him.

The woman walked in, standing looking at the two sat beside one another. "Now, what have I told you both?" she asked.

Billy shrugged. The girl looked away, trying to see where her phone had landed.

"I told you to play nice, but instead of that, it's time to get dressed now, you have school to go to."

"But Mum, it's holidays, we're off all week," the girl said.

The woman gave a panicked look, her eyes opening wide, as a pale appearance overtook her. She had forgotten.

"What, what time is it? What day is it?" the woman asked, sounding out of breath.

The girl giggled. "Got you, Mum," she called, laughing.

The woman looked down at the little girl with an expression of thunder. The very second she was about to shout, to scold her, a parent's natural empathy took over, and she changed just enough to matter.

"Abigail, don't do that, you had me in all of a panic."

Arthur listened to it all, her name, Abigail, it was a nice name, one that he remembered from before in his life but couldn't recall where from.

Abigail laughed again, but she knew, best not to be foolish over it. She stood up quickly, ran into the hall, grabbed her phone and went off again to her own room.

"Get dressed, clean your teeth, hurry up," the woman said.

Billy was once again lost in his own battle, moving soldiers all over, playing with this and that without a care in the world.

"Come on now, Billy, you know that means you too."

Billy looked up at her, all the while as Arthur watched on, wishing someone could love him that way.

"If you hurry I'll do you some porridge, with hot milk and plenty of sugar," the woman said, now smiling at him.

Billy smiled so wide his teeth showed. If Arthur ever tried to smile, to show his teeth in such a way, others would think he was being nasty and want to chase him away. Children could do such things and everyone would smile with them. Arthur wished he had been born a child, and wondered if they ever knew just how lucky they were. Provided they were loved like these children were.

Without any further prompting, Billy jumped up, surprising his mother and the little dog. He hastily began to dress as the woman left, ready to do what she had promised.

"Five minutes guys, breakfast and time for school."

Both children booed at the suggestion of school, but as always they knew there would be only one choice. Billy rushed to put on his jumper, the last of his uniform, before running out of his bedroom. He took one look at the bathroom, thought of cleaning his teeth, then decided he was too busy, and ran down the steep stairs. Countless times he had done what Arthur had done, gone crashing down and rolling around, but so far no broken bones.

Immediately following suit was Abigail, likewise in uniform. She took one step on the stairs, before realizing she needed to clean her teeth. She ran back to the bathroom, rubbed her gums with the brush, barely, before screaming down the stairs.

The noise and fuss continued, loud and cheerful as each tried to outdo the other. Arthur felt bold, that soon they would be gone. He lifted his head, but as he did a huge cry rang out from below. For a moment he thought he had been spotted.

"What's going on? What's all the fuss?" someone shouted. Now it was the man, wearing a smart suit, putting on a long, thin piece of cloth draped from his neck. He was stood in the hallway, looking down the stairs.

"What is this? What happened?" the voice came again from below. It was the woman, shouting about who knew what. Arthur knew, but he wasn't telling.

The man stormed down the stairs, charging to where the shouting was coming from. Abigail and Billy were stood at the doorway to the kitchen, looking in. Rubbish was strewn all over the floor, a mess of papers and plastic everywhere.

"Who did this?" the man asked loudly.

"I just asked that, thank you," the woman replied, glaring at him.

Both parents looked at the children, staring at them, with eyes that said *yes, you, you did it.*

Both children looked back with eyes that said *no, we didn't do it.*

"I didn't do it," Abigail said, getting her denial in first so that she could join the stares, looking at Billy, who must have done it.

Billy looked more shocked than ever. "I did not do that," he said, spelling out each and every word.

"Well whoever did it, you're both going to be grounded, no playing out tonight," Mother said.

"Awww, Mum," Billy shouted, before bursting into tears.

"It's not fair, I didn't do it, I shouldn't have to, you can't blame me..." Abigail scream storming off, stamping her feet.

It was a losing battle, and one neither parent could justify arguing. Mother began picking up the pieces, cleaning up.

"We don't have rats do we?" Father asked.

The moment he said the word, rats, Mother dropped the piece she had hold of, placed both hands in the air as if she were reaching for the sky and squealed. She stood back, her face a picture of despair.

"I'm not doing this if there are rats," she said, trying to walk away so carefully that she might have been walking on ice.

As soon as he saw it, Dad realized his mistake, he had said something which might have led to him having to clear it all up. The last thing he wanted to do.

"No, I'm sure there are none, maybe one of the kids sleepwalked," he said, walking out of the kitchen hastily. Before Mother could say a word he grabbed his bag from the hall.

"Sorry, can't stop, going to be late for work," he called, quickly leaving down the stairs.

Mother shrugged her shoulders. She had begun cleaning because she knew it would be left to her to deal with. She stopped a moment, aware of the time.

"Come on the pair of you," she said, walking out of the kitchen.

"I told you I didn't..." Abigail began.

"School, now," Mother said, not even bothering to look at her. She picked up both school bags and stood by the lounge door, holding them ready.

Billy grabbed his bag and ran down the stairs, as Abigail walked over to take hers. Her face made it clear she was angry, not happy at being blamed. She took the bag and left, following suit in a kind of march, as if she were walking in solidarity with her brother, united against the wrongs of the world.

As the back door closed, Mother sighed. Peace finally, as she readied to leave for work herself. She walked back into the kitchen, looked at the mess, thought of the rat, and decided to leave it, the man of the house could do it. She took her own bag, picked up her car keys and went out, deciding to ignore the problems, she would enjoy her day, and the house could take care of itself.

Little did she know that Arthur would do that for her.

CHAPTER THREE

All was quiet. Not even a bird made a sound. Arthur finally was alone. He had been fed, but badly needed the toilet, and sadly for him, he didn't know how to use the one right in front of where he lay. As always, he was peckish again and would have loved some food. Beside all of that, he was a bit bored, and fancied as much as anything to have some fun. Today, he figured, he would do all three.

First up, toilet break. Arthur ran out of Billy's bedroom, to the stairs and down. This time he felt brave, being alone, and went down the next flight of stairs. Immediately he saw the door he had entered through. His heart jumped at the thought of running around on the lovely grass outside, rubbing himself upside down on it, enjoying all the dirt and wet.

Sadly for him, the door was closed and locked. He could see through its glass panes, but had no idea how to get out. He jumped up at the door, pushing and scratching at it, wondering if a good rub at it might make it open. He pawed away at it for all his might, soft paws rubbing against the glass, but it refused to give.

Arthur dropped to the floor, resigned to not getting out. He looked around, seeing several doors, each one closed. There would be no escape that day. He didn't mind much, as he was still in love with his new home, but no matter, he had to relieve himself somehow.

He sprang back up the stairs, feeling ever more the need to go and relieve himself. He looked in the kitchen, then back out as he had already made his mark in there. Next up the door beside it. He went in and looked around. At the far end was almost an entire wall of windows, looking out onto the place he knew so well, all the streets and roads of the place he had spent years wandering around. Now he could see it all.

The room appeared inviting, soft furniture to sit on, covered in lovely white cushions, with a large rug sprawled across the middle of the floor. Several dark wooden units lined the wall, with a black oblong thing centered, which Arthur had seen before with moving pictures of other people on there, sometimes dogs. It was a bright airy room, a comfortable one to enjoy, where he would enjoy being able to see the world go by outside, without any of the risks. He would do so if only he could relieve himself; he needed a wee!

Arthur paced around, circling upon himself, desperately wondering what to do. One last thing, one more turn, then he spotted it. Sat at the side of the sofa was a tall green thing, like a bush, a plant that he recognized as the acceptable place to go. He rushed around the side of the sofa and looked it up and down. It sat in a large green pot, low to the ground, one he could easily reach. He sidled up to it, rubbed his body against the plant's large branches sticking out, looked once at the soil, did another circle and then smelled the soil again. It was great, just what he needed. He lifted his leg and finally got his release, as he did what needed to be done, watering the plants.

He waited, carrying on, and waited, and waited, until at long last he could breathe easily, letting out a long sigh of relief. The plant was watered, and he was satisfied. Job done.

What next?

Firstly, a look outside. He walked to the window, jumped onto his hind legs and leaned, front paws against the glass, looking out. It was amazing how much he could see, all those people milling around, the cars and buses, driving past so quickly, and none could honk their horns at him, none could try to run him down as so many seemed to try to do.

He could see a road he often traveled on, under the railway tracks. Before then, on the far side were some bushes leading right along the tracks. There he had often gone into to find a place to sleep, along with cats, mice, and insects. It had been busy in places like that, but still it wasn't as if he or any of the others had much choice. Now he did.

His head jerked this way and that, as if there was so much to see he couldn't quite take it all in. There was Bert, another dog, a golden Labrador, walking with his owner. He was fat and slow, the dog not the owner, because he was getting on in age. Still though, he was lucky, because he had an owner that cared about him. They would travel up St Peters Way several times during the day, and a couple more times during the night, just wandering along slowly, just in case Bert needed to go.

Then he saw Sally, the black cat, sat on a wall beside the railway bridge, high up. She was looking around, no doubt for some mice to play with, ok, actually to eat, but being nice and all, to enjoy some company with.

Her tail flicked all around, as if she were enjoying the moment, in the same way she seemed to enjoy it when he chased her, trying to get a hold of her tail. Just to play with, of course.

There was the local shop, where he would sometimes sit, in the hopes he would get some food scraps. Sometimes he did, but not always, at least not since the new owners went in and chased him away.

It was a sight to see, so high up, so much fun. Still though, it was time for food. If dogs could laugh Arthur would have done, because he was so foolish to think that there was a particular moment when it was food time. As if. Food time was all the time, every day, all day.

So food it would be.

He wandered back into the kitchen, looking amongst the wrappers on the floor. The pizza box was still there and he spent a moment licking the sauce leftovers from it. It wasn't as good as the night before, but not too bad. He looked around, before spotting a glass bowl on a worktop. In it sat several round things, orange colored, red and green. He knew from experience they didn't taste so great, not for a little dog anyway. At least they were there for if he couldn't find anything else.

It was time to turn his attention to his most prized part, his nose, that it might discover some tasty morsel that would keep him going until tea time, when the family came back. If they came back.

His nose gave mixed messages. It told him there was nothing easy to get at for food in the place he was stood, but no matter because it was also telling him there was food elsewhere. The faint aroma was calling his name, taunting him to follow and come play hide and seek.

Stop! Something else took over his needs, like most smelly dogs he had a problem, an instant problem, one that needed dealing with there and then: an itch! Arthur suddenly lunged at his tail, nibbling at it ferociously, as if it were some kind of snake attacking his bottom. Unfortunately, he wasn't the fittest of dogs and bending round to get a good bite at it wasn't easy. One front paw on the ground he pushed and pushed himself, lurching right over until he could just about reach, then snap, nibble and chew he went, going for it like his life depended on it.

Just one... more... push... one... more... nibble... and Arthur fell over backwards. He rolled around like one of the snails he enjoyed toying with, before twisting round and standing up. He stood there, looking sheepish, wondering if anyone had seen him make a fool of himself. Thankfully there wasn't. He breathed in, and sighed deeply, his chops flapping as he was so out of breath. He opened his mouth, breathing out a stream of hot steam, wondering if he should eat or just go and sleep some more. Tough choice.

A whiff of something tasty decided it for him and off he trotted to find it. It was like a trail of goodness, poking at his senses, not quite chocolate, not quite pizza, something in between. Instinctively he followed the trail, out into the hall, past the lounge, and to a new room he hadn't been in before. The door was pulled near closed, but he had enough about him to open a door, unlike some of the dogs he had known, who could hardly figure out how to open their own mouths.

As he walked through he noticed how full the room was, cuddly toys, balls to play with, a large oblong box on the wall like the one in the lounge, more soft furniture and toys everywhere, hundreds of them. As children went, these two were very lucky. So then was Arthur, because after food, and after sleep, there was nothing he liked more than playing!

Together his nose and his eyes focused on the prize, a plate in the corner, leftover food, pizza, some chips, but even better, chocolate too. Now dogs aren't supposed to eat chocolate, or peanuts, but then try telling that to a dog, especially one like Arthur. Dogs can't speak human, and even if Arthur could, he would just ignore you anyway because, well, he loves food!

So off he went, trotting across the room, when mid-walk a large thud from the floor below caught his attention. It was loud enough to make him stop walking, though not enough to make him stop thinking about the prize. He listened, and drooled, slobbering on himself, torn between danger and grub.

"I've just popped out, I'll be back in ten minutes, hold the report for me will you?" the voice asked, sounding quite familiar, if an unwanted distraction. Thudding noises of someone running up the stairs approached.

The same old panic returned, but Arthur was wary enough that he knew getting out of the room wasn't an option. He looked ahead, wondering if he could hide behind the furniture, but no, it was only bean bags, children's ones, and none big enough to hide him and his big fat bottom.

Should he dive out and run down the stairs, hoping the outside door was open? If he did, it would mean leaving such a comfy home, but who would want to do that? Should he go and say hello, wagging tail and licking their hands, giving them a warm welcome and insisting he was a new member of the family? He had tried that in the past and found people usually returned the welcome with a quick scream and a swift kick.

Completely out of options, Arthur leaped over to the pile of cuddly toys, burrowing into them. As he did the pile spilled over, so that it was no longer a pile but instead a mess of toys spread out all over. He turned and sat, looking at the doorway, surrounded by a mass of white, pink, blue and red teddies, fluffy toys and all sorts in between. It was over, the fun, the food, the warmth, the comfort. Soon, the shouting would begin.

He just sat, looking, waiting for them to come in and see him.

The lady of the house walked past, holding a large bag in one hand, a cell phone in the other. Arthur simply waited.

As seconds ticked by Arthur began to shake, afraid of what was to come. He never liked being in difficult situations, but it was the story of his life. Sooner or later everything went wrong for him.

"Yeah, I just can't find the report, I left it here this morning, but for the life of me I can't see it," the lady of the house said again, walking around, before entering the games room, standing right inside the doorway, looking in.

Arthur just stared at her, any second, waiting for the response.

Mother looked on, holding onto her phone to her ear, looking out of the window, directly towards Arthur's direction.

"What, seriously? I came all this way only for you to find it there after all?" she asked, her face a look of anger. She turned around and stormed out, down the stairs, out of the back door, locking it before disappearing again. Arthur continued to sit, staring at the doorway, wondering just what happened.

Finally, he looked around himself, struggling to comprehend that she had seen only cuddly toys, and thought he was one. As if anyone could mistake him for being cuddly, or a toy.

Life was strange sometimes, as much for people as for dogs, but when good things happened the best thing to do was accept them. Arthur did, walking over the cuddly toys to the plate. He was in no mood to savor it, instead just opening wide and devouring it all. He almost choked on one particularly large slice of pizza, but he was a trooper, he could cope, and managed to down it all in one go.

The chocolate was nice, a little chewy as it had a toffee center, but still very welcome, if a little naughty. His tummy sent back the message that it was happy, and so it was time for some fun. Things had been good so far that day, and for once in his life he could relax in a way that didn't involve sleeping.

He took one look at the spread of toys and dived in, lunging at one particularly large toy, a white, fluffy, round bear. It had big floppy ears and a cute nose. Arthur grabbed at one of its ears, taking a good, quick hold of it and ran, springing this way and that, rolling around on the floor, before diving back at it again, biting his head, gently, not mean, but in a playful way, rolling all over it as if he were a puppy again and were fighting one of his brothers or sisters. Like he did when he was young, but hadn't for a long time.

It was a battle of wits, as the teddy bear looked on at him like some rogue figure bent on taking over the world, it challenged him as it sat there flopped over, its soft fur like a red flag to a bull. He charged at it, grabbing its ears again before tumbling right over, round and round. The pair were a spectacle, tumbling around and play grabbing, except the bear was just there, a toy, doing nothing, it was the little dog doing it all, but that didn't matter, to him he was having fun and frolics with his equal in every way.

Puffing and panting, finally Arthur gave up. He had won his play battle, and he was in charge. His head was covered in bits of white fur, but so too was the carpet, except that also had a white ear on it, with bits of filling all over, yellow pieces of foam here and there.

Arthur laid on his side, feeling the newly arrived warm sun coming flooding in. It was lovely on his fur, making him so warm and relaxed, all he wanted to do was sleep. His tummy was full, he was tired from all the exertions, and it was quiet and restful. Perfect.

He drifted off into the land of nod, his tiny mind wandering to places and people he had known before. Street dogs like him have very varied and different lives, but not always easy, not to say of being broken up from your mother and father at a very early age, as well as no longer seeing your brothers and sister ever again. It was sad for some, but most went into loving homes and loving lives and made the most of it. Some like Arthur never found that, pushed here and there, wandering all over, rarely feeling proper affection. He could dream about it though.

In his dream, he was much taller but not quite so smelly, though he didn't even know he was anyway. He had friends, another female dog called Sasha, as well as good owners. That morning he was laid in his dreams in bed, near his adult mother, as she did her knitting. She would use her foot on him, rubbing his side, making him feel loved, and whenever he woke up she would drop a morsel of food his way, which he would gobble up and get back to relaxing again.

Then another dog, one that was really him as he was, would come along and bark at him, telling him not to be so silly, not to believe that he was so lucky. That was when the yelping began, for real, his dreams would come out in yelps and chirping noises, little calls as his eyes fluttered, telling us all he was dreaming. Sometimes his dreams would be nice, and some not so nice, and that day his dream wasn't so nice.

That was the lives of dogs, some of them at least. Like Arthur.

CHAPTER FOUR

The key turned, and Abigail pushed open the door. She was on autopilot, finish morning school, home for lunch, walk the usual way, go around the back way, make sure she had her key, unlock the door, open it, go in. It was the same routine, five days a week, to afternoon television that had nothing worth watching and food which was never heated because there was no one in to cook it. It was a routine she was used to, and one she had many more years of looking forward to.

She was young, but not so young that she couldn't be trusted with a key, or keys as it turned out. She had been given a key, months ago, but of course lost it, never to be seen again. Her second key was given to her on the understanding that she would be ever-so-careful over it, and treasure it as precious, that she would never lose it or a Unicorn would take away her mobile phone. Being too old to believe such a thing, she lost the key the very next day. Finally, she was given the key she had now, and told if she lost it then she would get no more pocket money for a full year. Five months later she still had the key.

Her bag of books, pens, and bits dropped to the floor as if it had been a lead weight around her neck, and she began the annoying ascent up the stairs to the annoying food and boring television. At least if she ate quickly she could read a little or play with something. Abigail had a total of thirty minutes to eat and do before she had to go again back to the *worst play in the world*: school.

She pulled open the fridge door and leaned in, looking around. There was half a chicken, but Mum had said eat that and she would get no tea. There was cheese, but that was fattening. Not so good. Finally, she spotted a plate of sandwiches, tuna and cucumber for a change, except that was always what they were because she wouldn't eat anything else.

Abigail took the sandwiches from the fridge, closed the door and looked at the pile of papers and wrappers strewn across the floor. She was thankful she wasn't going to be the one to pick it all up, but was annoyed Billy was like he was, so messy.

The sandwiches tasted OK, not so fresh and a little wet, but she was hungry anyway. She walked out, heading to the games room to sit on a bean bag chair, before changing her mind at the last minute. She headed into the lounge, looked around and wondered about playing a video game, before real-life and the time limits it brought reminded her of what she had no choice but to do.

No matter, she left again, mouth full of tuna, chewing away, enjoying it even if she wouldn't admit to it. She headed into the games room, stopping at the last minute, wondering what the smell was. A foul odor had finally overwhelmed the smell of her sandwiches, and she sniffed, much like Arthur was fond of doing, only as she did so she scrunched up her face, wondering why something smelled so bad.

"What is that smell?" she asked the air around her.

The voice was enough to alert Arthur, who immediately opened his eyes, realizing he had been sound asleep, still on his side, still in the sunshine, in the middle of the games room floor. He had gone soft, in the space of a few hours, he had forgotten all that life had taught him, about people, and what could happen.

A cough nearby made him jump, as he looked up to see Abigail stood in the doorway. She held onto a plate of something fine, which she was enjoying a great deal, but was looking back into the hall, sniffing around. He wondered if she might be searching out for more food like he had, that maybe he should go and join her and they could sniff and search together.

Silly idea.

There was an open door to hide behind, some bean bag chairs to possibly lay under, the cuddly toys but they had been spread out all over, no longer in a pile since he had crashed into them. He could stand still again and see if she realized he should be there, or just run. It was all too much to think of, and once again he felt the panic rising. He looked one way, then the next, then at her, before running straight towards her.

Abigail turned to enter the room, just as he had run to her. She looked into the room, wondering where to sit, when her attention immediately focused on the bits of teddy all over. It was like the kitchen, messy.

'You're slipping, Mum, not keeping the place tidy. That's your job,' she thought, finishing the last of her sandwiches.

Arthur ran past her legs, so nimbly she barely even felt his presence. She was too taken up by munching on her food, her mind on her usual routine, looking for something to make the day different, never mindful that a dog might have managed to get into their home and be hiding there.

Out he went into the hall, as Abigail walked into the room, went to sit on a bean chair, before realizing she had forgotten something.

"Duh, drink," she said, turning around again.

Arthur was stood in the hall, at a crossroads between looking at the last of her food and where to hide, or even if he should. His choice was made up for him as he saw the girl come back out, turning to head for the kitchen again. He didn't wait around to be seen, his heart pounding as he shot quietly back up the stairs. He had no time to think, she could be chasing him, could have seen him, anything. He got to the top and ran straight ahead, barging through the door to a room he had never seen.

A thudding sound interrupted Abigail's thoughts, as she was halfway through a mouthful of 7-Up from a can. It was loud enough not to have been something outside. She knew the area, had been there all her life, and how safe her house and the place was, but still, she was curious and still concerned.

Time was short, not enough to sit and watch anything, so instead she would go to her room to see if anything provoked an interest in there, or at least anything she could take to school to alleviate the boredom of another maths lesson. She headed for the stairs.

Arthur was in the alien room, a place he had never seen and didn't understand. He looked all around, jerking his head like a parrot trying to see something that was never there. In one corner sat a large set of drawers, beside them a small stool and a desk in front of it with a mirror, one with a dog looking back at him in blind panic. A wooden bed ran the length of one wall, with drawers in it and a gap underneath. There were cushions scattered around, and posters of odd-looking people in strange colors, posing, but not much else, small boxes, a lamp stood in a corner with a pink shade.

'Baby you light up my world like nobody else,' the voice cried. Abigail was singing, but Arthur had no clue that was what it was supposed to be. To him, it sounded like shouting, as if she were after him.

'The way that you flip your hair gets me overwhelmed,' she continued, her footsteps sounding muffled but thumping on the carpet as she walked down the hall.

Now it really was time to panic. He imagined her coming straight in, seeing him, screaming and running for a big stick. He didn't like sticks.

In a mad dash, he pushed over the stool and headed straight for the gap under the bed. Head down, front legs at the ready he leaped as hard as he could, pushing himself under the narrow gap. It was too late to realize he wouldn't fit, better to wedge himself in than have someone scream at him. He pushed and pushed and scratched with his claws with all his might to try and get in. Bit by bit he felt his body going further, first his head, then his neck, then his shoulders, then... his bottom wouldn't fit, no matter what he did. It was dark underneath, and he just hoped as much as a dog can hope, that it would be enough.

'But when you smile at the ground it ain't hard to tell,' Abigail continued, singing her heart out, finally finding something to enjoy about the day with a song she loved. The first thing she noticed was the stool knocked over, on its side and in the way of her dressing table. She took hold of the bottom edge and turned it over, dropping it heavily down. She plonked herself down on the stool, looking into the mirror, before grabbing a brush for her hair and continuing to sing.

Arthur just sat, bottom sticking up in the air, tail not daring to wag. His face was covered in fluff and dust, unable to see a thing. He couldn't help but shake, he was so nervous. There was nothing else he could do but wait, and listen to her sing.

A buzzing sound interrupted both Abigail's singing and his shaking.

"Oh, gonna be late," she called, before turning and running from the room, heading off downstairs. Arthur waited, wondering if it was all clear, when suddenly she burst back in, grabbed keys off the desk and ran again. He listened as she grabbed hold of her bag, went out of the door, slamming it, locking it behind her.

It was silent again, finally he was all alone. His shaking subsided a little, enough for him to allow himself to think a bit about what he was going to do. He reversed his stance, trying with all his might to pull himself back out from under the bed. He pushed and pushed and scraped the carpet, until his body moved out a little, except his fur and scrunched up skin remained stuck tightly in place. He stopped, feeling very awkward, wondering if he was missing a trick. He wasn't the smartest of dogs, but instinctively he was able to find a way to do most things. Not this time.

He tried shifting sideways, left, then right, turning a little, pulling again, pushing some more. Nothing worked. Anyone outside watching him would have laughed so hard, seeing a large brown fur bottom moving all over, listening to his struggle. No doubt feeling sorry for him too.

There was nothing else for it, it was simply time for the thing that always got him out of scrapes when push came to shove:

panic! He suddenly began pushing, pulling, turning, scraping all over, acting like a wound spring that had just snapped, scrambling like some mad thing so much that the bed rocked, the carpet moved and the stool once again went flying.

With a huge plop, Arthur shot free, so hard that he fell upon his hind legs, almost standing up, before falling back into the wall behind. He laid back, all four paws sticking up in the air, looking around as if he were a baby in a crib, waiting for his bottle.

It had been a crazy day, and all he could think of was to get somewhere safe. Righting himself, Arthur walked out of the room, back into Billy's, and into the welcoming home that was the darkness under his bed. It was warm, quiet, and unlikely anyone would trouble him there. He crawled to the corner, pulled himself round into a tightly wound coil, and fell once again into a deep sleep.

CHAPTER FIVE

"No, I want it, Dad, you said I could have it," Billy shouted.

"No, I said you could have it first, then me, then Abigail, then Mum," Dad said, looking at Billy as he struggled with his key to the door.

"Hey, hold on, you said me!" Abigail shouted, until all three were shouting, trying to be heard over the other.

"Stop!" a voice louder than any of them demanded. Nobody would argue with Mum, she was in charge.

All three silenced, looking at her as she entered through the door. "Now, everyone go in, get cleaned up, and rest until tea is ready," she said, not bothering to wait for an answer. There would only be one answer anyway.

The family took off their coats, hung up bags and made their way upstairs. Abigail headed for her room, Billy to his, and Dad, well he tried, but failed.

"Er, Stan, not so fast, you're with me, we're going to clean the kitchen, sort that mess out," Mum said. She turned her back on him, continuing to walk towards the kitchen, ignoring anything he might do or say. As it was he simply pulled a face, horrified at the thought of cleaning. He thought of trying to make the case that cleaning was a woman's work, but he knew even if he was joking after a long day at work she might not see the funny side of it.

Billy ran up to his room, bursting through the door so loud that he even managed to wake Arthur. Billy was excited to play, but couldn't decide whether to watch children's TV, play with his action figures, or do something else. He loved his toys, but especially when he had things he could do something with, such as building with Meccano or Lego bricks. His parents, being sensible people, didn't overdo it. He didn't have a mobile phone, not like Jack, his friend next door, and he only had enough toys to play with, but still, life was good and he was happy.

It would be fire engine day he decided, pulling out his large, bright red fire engine. Next up he grabbed a plastic tub full of various stick-like figures, brightly painted, along with various signs and pieces to complement the scene.

He looked around, struggling to see the thing he most wanted.

"Muuuuum," he shouted. No reply came.

"Muuuuuuuuum," he shouted as loud as he could.

"Billy, stop making all that noise," Abigail called back.

"I don't want you, I want Mum," Billy replied.

"I don't want you either, but I'm stuck with you," came the ill-considered response.

Billy ignored her. Just as he was about to shout again, he was stopped in his tracks.

"What is it? I'm busy." It was his mother calling.

"I can't find my fire engine playhouse, where is it?" Billy asked.

"I haven't touched it, try looking under your bed with the rest of the contents of the house."

It seemed like the only option, but not one he wanted. He knew there might be spiders and other creepy crawlies under there, not to mention grotty dust which made him sneeze, and smelly clothes too. It was the last place he wanted to explore, but without a fire station he couldn't put out any fires. He had no choice.

There was no way he was going to put his hand under there, it was dark, plus there might be scary clowns and bogeymen under there ready to grab him. He sat and thought for a moment, wondering what he might do. He thought of asking Abigail but she would most likely make fun of him for being scared, and besides she might want something in exchange, like some of his sweets next time they got some. As if.

An idea struck Billy, as he jumped up and ran down the stairs. Arthur continued to lay in the darkness, but watched everything he did, mindful of something happening that he might not like.

Footsteps came running down the hall as Billy burst back in, holding a sweeping brush. The moment he entered Arthur lifted his head, fully aware that something was going on, something that he might not like.

Billy pushed the brush end under his bed, and stopped. He was thinking, what if he dragged on something, and pulled out a pile of old washing and his mum saw it, or worse, a giant spider crawled out and leaped on him. It gave him the shivers.

There was no way he could properly play without it, but sister, mum, and dad weren't going to help, so it was the brush. He would do it carefully, and if anything came out that shouldn't he would either push it right back, or up and run screaming as loud as he could. With any luck, he thought, he would get away and it would take his sister instead.

Slowly does it, Billy edged the brush under. As he did so Arthur looked intently at it, unseen, hidden in his little hole, but wary all the same. He could see the bristles along the far edge of the bed, as they slowly crawled towards him. He tried to lift himself up, in case he needed to sprint away, but the bed was in the way. He could crawl out again, but being so low he couldn't move quickly enough to get away. All he could do was push back towards the wall and hope he wasn't spotted.

Billy hooked onto something, gradually pulling it out. It was a toy car, larger than he wanted, and besides it had a pair of bright yellow underpants stuck to it, which he certainly didn't want to play with. He used the brush to lift them off, pushing them back where they belonged, firmly in the land of forgotten.

Next up, he tried further along. It was slow and boring doing it, so he tried a good hard shove. With any luck, it would knock out any monsters under there, and at the same time he could magically find his fire station. It would drop out for him, just like that.

The end of the brush jammed into Arthur's large bottom, making him jump. As he did he bumped his head on the soft underside of the bed. It didn't hurt, but it wasn't nice. Something was going to have to give. He continued to watch the boy, as he pushed and prodded with his brush.

Finally, Billy latched onto something much bigger, that wasn't underpants, cars or dog, and began to gently pull it back out. Even though he hadn't caught Arthur while fishing, it still panicked him, as he tried to move away and found there was no way to go. The brush stuck on the hidden object and Billy pulled harder, tugging at its stick, jerking it until it seemed to give. Each jab caught Arthur, making him more and more nervous. Something had to give.

Arthur crawled away from the wall, towards the edge of the bed, desperate to avoid the big stick. Just as his nose popped out from under the bed Billy gave one more almighty pull, as the bed finally let go of the fire station, sending the boy rolling back as the station flew and hit the wall behind him. A plate joined it, covered in fluff and green mold. Arthur shot out, flying out of the door unseen, into the hall. Fleeing like a fox, he looked all around, nobody in sight, down the stairs he went. At the bottom were both parents, at the end of the hall in the kitchen, rubber gloves on, sorting rubbish. Panic again as he ran, back down another flight of stairs, into darkness below. Night had fallen, and with it another place to hide.

"Billy, was that you?" his mother called. No answer. Finally, after looking, wondering what she had seen, his mother decided to find out for herself.

She very much expected some kind of order in the house, especially with two young children around. She was a busy woman, loved by the family, but tough when she needed to be. She particularly preferred Stan to call her by her first name, Nancy, not Mum or Mother like the children did, but she wondered at times if he had ever grown up properly.

"Hey, what about..." Stan tried to argue, annoyed at having to wear gloves, but more annoyed at having to clean up rubbish.

"Billy," she called.

"Yeah," Billy shouted. It was obvious he was upstairs. She began to wonder what she had seen, if anything.

Nancy walked over to the top of the stairs, looking down. She felt tired, still wearing her office clothes, a white blouse and black skirt, all she could think about was getting sorted and enjoying a long soak in the bath.

"Abigail," she called.

"What, Mum?" Abigail called back, also clearly from above.

Arthur had stopped at the bottom of the lower stairs, and was looking through the window of the door he had entered through. No matter how comfy the place was, how nice the food was, he had had enough, he just wanted to get out and be free of it all.

Footsteps once more interrupted his ideas of escape, right behind him, coming down to him. He was too scared to wait to be let out, he needed to run, anywhere.

Several doors stood around him, one a smaller half-size one, the other two white wooden, and apparently closed. Arthur ran across the small hall, his nails clicking on the hard tiles.

"Who's down there?" Nancy called, slowing her walk, nervous at there being something or someone down there, but uncertain what it could be. She wondered whether to call Stan, but she knew he would call the police, and then it could be a lot of fuss for very little. It was either that, or go find out. She was tired, so just decided to go for it.

Now or never, Arthur knew he was trapped. It was all about to kick off.

CHAPTER SIX

Nancy's footsteps were soft on the stair carpet, with her plush slippers masking her descent, but Arthur could still tell she was coming. He had a super-refined sense of smell, from years of needing to find food anywhere, but also from the scent and warmth of approaching people and animals on the street, where anything could happen. He knew from earlier it was the mother, her fine fragrance, and the warmth she gave off, instinctively he could tell she was a nice person, but even the nicest people reacted funny when they found a stray dog in their homes.

Arthur looked around frantically, as if he were doing an impression of a chicken trying to escape its fate. He looked this way and that, up and down, for all the good it would do him. He could see legs appearing on the last stairs, about to see him. Panicked, unable to think straight, he headed for the nearest door, the half one, but firmly closed, then the other white one, closed too, as he scratched at it frantically. Finally, he shot over to the last door, scratched several times at it, as it opened, just enough for him to shoot through, disappearing into the darkness.

"Hello, is there anyone there? Please speak now, or forever hold your peace," Nancy said, not entirely seriously. She didn't know whether there really was anything or anyone down there, or if it was just her mind playing tricks, but it had been a long day at work.

She looked ahead, looked out into the garden as early evening lights began to come on in the streets outside. Just as she was about to go back up she felt a flush of cool air, and wondered where it was from. The part open door was clearly to blame, and so she walked over to close it.

Nancy stopped, peeked her head inside, felt the cold and noted the darkness, before deciding against going down the steps. It was too late and far too cold to bother with whatever was going on. She just closed the door with a click and went back upstairs to the family, chores, and food that everyone was waiting for. It was tough being expected to provide so much, but still no matter what, for her, family was worth it.

It all went quiet as Arthur stood in the darkness, at the top of the steps. He stared into the nothing, wondering if any moment the woman would come back and open the door. Maybe she was aware he was there and just messing with him. Maybe it was a game. He would wait a while and see, and though he was experienced with how things could be for a lonely little dog, he never ever lost his optimism and hope, such was his loving nature. Except for cats, which he thought only existed to be chased.

Time went by and still he waited, as the cold air began to remind him he was no longer in the warmth of the house. Slowly but surely he came to realize that no one was coming back for him, for good or bad. He crept forward, struggling to see anything ahead. He became aware of where he was as he bumped his head on the side of the door, but he wasn't bothered by it, he had a hard head.

Arthur lifted his paw scratching gently at it. He figured one of these kind people would hear his polite calling using his paw and come to the rescue. Nobody did. He scratched again, and then again, then a few more times with both paws. It was a thick door and no one heard a thing.

Unsure of what to do, Arthur turned around and looked ahead, seeing only vague shadows dance around him. He walked as slowly as he could ahead, feeling his way, realizing there were steps, and began to descend down them.

Unlike most children, Arthur wasn't afraid of the dark, but he hated the cold and hated being hungry. Sadly for him, that was what he was getting right then and there, both.

He walked down the thin wooden stairs, one after the other. As he went down it became colder and colder. Whatever happened he wouldn't be able to sleep there, he knew it. He would have to escape.

Finally, he hit rock bottom, literally, as a smooth, hard and cold floor became obvious under his paws. He could see a light coming from a large oblong object in a corner, just enough to make out the place. There were boxes all round with sheets and covers across them. Beyond that he couldn't see much of it so turned to his trusty friend, his nose. He began sniffing the air, his head bobbing up and down as he did so, looking like he was swimming in the atmosphere.

A faint but positive aroma caught his attention, as the possibility of food struck him. Whatever it was, it would take his mind off the cold for now.

Lowering his head he began to sniff the floor, occasionally twisting and turning to follow the scent. As he approached the oblong object his nose sniffed up a long pile of fluff and he began to sneeze, quietly at first, then more until he seemed like an elephant trying to cough up an armchair.

Eventually, he cleared the worst of it, once again continuing his food hunt. His nose took him to a corner of the cold, damp room, until he could just about make out a small pile of something. He nudged it with his dripping nose, wondering if it might move. It didn't, so he sniffed it some more, before nudging it. Finally, it was time, as he opened his mouth and slobbered a lick on it, wondering if it would be good or bad. It was neither, but it smelt edible, so off he went, biting it quickly, before picking it up with his mouth. It was dirty, didn't smell so great and was more than a little moist, but unbeknown to him he was eating a moldy potato. Quite edible, if a little rotten.

As meals went it wasn't the best, but it wasn't the worst he had tried. So Arthur stood in the dark, except for a little green light, eating a moldy potato, his nose dripping, beginning to shiver with the cold.

As he finished he let out a great loud burp, releasing nasty gases from his stomach. It was nasty, but he wanted more and began sniffing again. Quickly he found another dusty, dirty potato and began nibbling away. It was a feast, one fit not for a king but a peasant, but it was something.

Arthur could feel his stomach rumbling, not from hunger but from the effects of his new meal. He waited, expecting to burp again, but instead wind came out of his other end, lending a foul odor to the room. He wasn't a fussy dog, but even he could tell it was bad. For now, he wouldn't be sniffing the air again for a while.

His shivering grew worse, such was the cold. It was too much to bear so he found his way again up the cellar stairs. It was darker upstairs, but not as cold. Blocking his way was a big, hard door which wasn't going away soon. There was no alternative, he would just have to call for help.

"What time is tea, love?" Stan asked as he sat in his favorite chair, reading the newspaper, television on, waiting for the football to come on. It had been a long busy day at work, and he was doing what he enjoyed most: relaxing.

"I don't know, love, why don't you go find out, love," Nancy replied, returning a sarcastic look.

"Yeah, Dad, go get it yourself, love," Abigail piped up. He looked at her, astonished, wondering how such a thing was possible.

"Hey we'll have less of that," Nancy said, giving a stern look that she meant it.

"Yeah Abigail, love, do..." Billy began to say.

"Enough," Nancy shouted, finally standing up. She had heard enough, and figured if she left it nobody would get fed.

"Sorry lo... er I mean Nancy, let me help," Stan said, trying to stand up while dropping his newspaper. Nancy ignored his pleas, walking out of the lounge to the kitchen.

"How about a nice spaghetti Bolognese, mince, pasta, sauce, mushrooms, cheese, potatoes. Doesn't that sound ace?" Stan asked, imagining it in his mouth as he spoke.

"We don't have any mushrooms," Nancy replied as they both walked into the kitchen.

"Oh, OK, no mushrooms then, but."

"We don't have any sauce either."

"Oh."

"Or mince."

"Oh."

"Or pasta."

"Right. Do we have any food at all?" Stan asked, immediately regretting it.

"Of course, we have potatoes for chips, and we have frozen fish in the freezer, and we would have had more in if you had spent less time on television and more time shopping with me," Nancy insisted, pulling out food from the freezer. Stan imagined several possible answers to her point, but none of them would improve her mood, so he just decided food prep was the best thing and less chat.

"Did you call?" Billy asked, wandering into the kitchen.

"No, I'm busy preparing food," Stan said. Nancy looked at him as if her look could freeze a sand dune, he stood motionless, waiting for a tirade that never came.

Billy turned around to walk out, stopping mid-walk to look around.

"One of you called my name," Billy insisted.

"I didn't," Nancy said, dropping a large bag of frozen chips onto the counter.

"Oh no, not frozen chips, again," Billy said loudly.

"Oh Mum, I'm sick of them," Abigail said traipsing into the kitchen. She looked forlorn, as if her world had suddenly ended.

"Oh yes, that's all we have because your dad didn't buy anything in," Nancy said, fully aware that the blame was shared, but in no mood to accept any part in it.

Stan looked at her as if she had forgotten he was stood next to her.

"There it is again, that noise, calling my name," Billy said, looking out into the hall.

"Stan, would you please go and see what he's on about," Nancy asked. It was a question, but sounded more like an order.

Stan was glad to be able to escape the scene of his problems, if only for a few moments.

"Where is this coming from, Billy?" Stand asked. "Come and show me."

"I'm hungry," Billy replied, which meant there would be no further discussion about it, he was on his own.

A long, quiet but withering sound pricked Stan's ears, just loud enough to gain his attention but not enough to bother anyone else. It was hardly surprising to him that no one else went with him, especially when food was a consideration.

The noise stopped, leaving him wondering if it was just the wind outside. As he walked to the edge of the stairs he looked out of the window, seeing how poor the weather had become. Brown leaves were swirling around en masse, as heavy wind swept it all up into a basket of fury. He looked at the gray sky and shivered. Even though the house was lovely and warm inside, he could just imagine how cold it must have become. He was glad he was indoors away from it all.

Stan stood for a moment, wondering whether to bother. Just as he was about to turn, a shrill high pitched whine made him look around, trying to gather where it was coming from. It was a long sound, hollow but sad. He would have to go down and find out what was going on, such were the joys of being the man of the house.

The noise changed to scratching, sounding as if it were coming from the back door. He wondered if something had fallen against the door, wind moving it around. The last thing he needed was broken glass in the door pane so down he would go.

As he walked down it was clearly much colder. Used for storage and getting in and out, he had turned off the lower heating and the difference was stark.

Stan flicked the ground hall switch, lighting the place up just enough to see. He loved the LED lights, but had somehow convinced himself how good they were even if they were so dim he could hardly see properly. The main thing was saving electricity.

A short sniffing sound came again, only this time from one of the internal doors. It sounded as if the door itself were making sounds, which while odd was also unsettling. Slowly Stan walked across the hall, listening intently, trying to work out which one if was coming from. It wasn't the small door, nor the full-size one to the cupboard, it was the one to the cellar. He had visions of opening the door to see a pile of rats looking up at him, as if he were the Pied Piper, ready to lead them on a merry dance.

He placed his hand on the cold handle, steeling himself for the worst. He wondered for a second whether to call for reinforcements, but decided he couldn't cope with the looks they would give him for being a little afraid, and besides, nobody would come anyway if he called. He could smell the food wafting from upstairs, wondering if he should just go and forget about it. Before he could make his choice the sniffing sound came again, followed by the patter of something on the steps inside.

It was now or never. Just in case, he walked quickly over to the back door, opened it up and let in a torrent of cold air. It was a bad idea, but anyway, if it were rats, they would have somewhere to go.

Stan grabbed the handle, turned and opened it inwards. As he pushed, something on the other side knocked against leading to a thumping sound as something dropped down the stairs. In his mind, it was confirmed, rats, or snakes, or a pack of wild creatures wanting to attack him the moment he stepped through.

Common sense took over and he walked in, head held high, daring to look down. He lifted his hand into the air, fumbling around to find the light cord. The smell of the place reminded him why he hardly ever went down, because it was dark, cold and smelly. The last place he wanted to be.

Stan stopped for a moment, listening, twisting his head around for signs of noise. There was nothing, just silence, as if silence could be a sound, it did to him, seeming odd and out of place. It would be all junk, covered in sheets, and dust, which he was allergic to.

Whatever he thought, he would have to go and find out what had caused the fuss. He finally caught hold of the light and pulled, bringing with it a stream of poorly lit white to the stairs, but little else. He began to descend, imagining himself like a British Indiana Jones, searching out snakes and treasure.

As he walked further down the light faded, and for the hundredth time he cursed himself for not doing something about it every single time he had been in there. At the bottom, it felt much quieter, no noise from the house, no wind outside, and apart from the smell, all seemed settled. He looked around as best he could, trying to make out movement in the shadows. There was nothing, just himself and a ton of unused and forgotten possession that should have been thrown out long ago, including all the baby toys that Nancy would never ever part with.

A sudden noise caught his attention, the sound of escaping air, whistling as it did. For a moment he thought it was a gas pipe, making his heart pound with concern. He thought to run and shout everybody out, but as he was about to something affected him, stopped him in his tracks. Far from a disturbing smell of leaking gas, another profoundly awful smell took a hold of his nose, telling him that all was not right. It was like a cross between rotten meat and dirty pond water. Immediately Stan held his nose, choking back tears as the whiff made him almost dizzy with its vile nature.

"Awwww, no," he said, staggering back a little.

He looked around again, still holding his nose, wishing there had been a window to open. He looked at a pile of boxes, covered in a large dustsheet. Whatever it was, it was worth leaving until he could find a torch.

As he walked over to begin the climb up the stairs, something moved quickly within the darkness, scuttling along like a shadow on wheels. Stan had no chance, as the thing moved underneath him just as he was about to step forward. His foot caught on it as it slid along, swiping his balance away, forcing him to upend and fall. The world fell over as everything spun, arms out he dropped to the ground with a thud. The ground was cold and dirty, much worse than he had even thought. He waited a moment, wondering if any pain might suddenly present itself to him, but nothing, he was alright, if a little embarrassed.

Then the thought struck him of the giant rat that had just tripped him. He turned over quickly, trying to see what was going on, if it was after him. Panic set in.

Before Stan could fully turn over, Arthur, having almost been crushed, rushed away from the fallen man, heading straight for the stairs, running as fast as he could up them. If he had been able, he would have slammed the door behind himself, and if the back door had been open he would surely have bolted out and away. Warm and comfy as it may have been, the house was no place for a stray dog. Far too much trouble.

Arthur scrambled away, ignoring anything behind him, all that mattered was getting away. All he could see as he ran was the way ahead, looking for the next door, the next path, any way he could find to get away. Doors were all closed, all there was were stairs, up. Back he went, scrambling with all his might, up the carpeted stairs to the next floor. As he got to the top, breathless, he looked down the hall, to see the woman of the house, carrying a tray of food through the doorway. He wondered if he might run up to her and sit quickly, holding out a paw, that she might be kind and drop a bowl to the floor and rub the top of his head. From experience in the past, trying just such a thing, it would never happen. It usually resulted in a scream, bowls dropped to the floor, and before he could lick anything up he would feel a sweeping broom on his bottom while being chased around a room.

Nancy looked ahead of herself, walking carefully so as not to trip or drop anything. Much as she disliked the children eating in the lounge, she would let them every now and then, and this was it. Friday night, fish and chips, in the warmth, together. She couldn't say no. From the corner of her eye, she caught sight of something moving, but as she looked it was gone, in a flash, a blur that but from the briefest moment meant nothing. The children were hungry, that was all that mattered. As usual, Stan was nowhere to be seen.

Arthur fled up yet more stairs, not taking any chances. He scurried away, breathless now, not used to so much running up stairs. He got to the top, saw the room with the hidden space all for him and dived in, underneath the bed. He scrambled on all fours, pulling himself to safety. As he did, and for the first time, he noted the awful smell. He didn't need to know where it was coming from, it was his own bottom. Whatever he had eaten in the cellar, it was playing havoc with his tummy.

Stan walked into the lounge, and immediately both children burst out laughing, pointing to him.

"Why are you so dusty, Dad?" Billy cried, laughing with a mouth full of chips.

"Billy, don't laugh at your dad with your mouth full," Nancy said.

"Yeah Billy, finish your chips then laugh at him," Abigail said, giggling away to herself.

"Abigail, don't say that, but yes Billy, swallow then laugh," Nancy said, joining in the laughter.

Stan was stood in the doorway, covered in thick dust, his hair a wild mop of cobwebs and debris. His face looked a picture, amazement, surprise, and annoyance. It looked as if he were lost, unable to speak and in dire need of a good wash.

"Dinner's ready," Nancy said, as the three burst out laughing. Stan just looked at her, not the least amused.

"I have no idea what that was, it could be a rat, but it got away and could be upstairs," Stan said succinctly, before walking out. He may be the butt of their jokes, but at least they could experience some of the fun he had been having. As he walked out he heard Abigail cry out, and the three of them begin to shout and jump around.

"Rats!" was the common word between them. Of course, he didn't believe it, he hadn't seen any, and had fallen over himself, but he would let them stew a little, before telling them the truth.

CHAPTER SEVEN

It was totally dark. Arthur was surrounded by old socks, fluff, and a wall, and there was nothing to touch him, nothing at all to worry him. He was at peace, and alone. It was time to drift off to wonderland.

As the darkness drifted away, instead of being under a boy's bed, he was in a field, full of long grass. Someone nearby was calling his name, Arthur, shouting to him. Her voice was so soft, so full of love and fun. He was running, bounding through the grass, each leap to try to see her smile, the look of joy and love on her face and in her eyes.

The skies were pure blue, the sun was warm and fine, and the air was just enough to ruffle his ears and nothing more. His coat was shiny brown, reflecting the colors of the flowers as he ran around them. His teeth were all sharp and white, well-tended, used to large meals of meat and bones. It showed.

Arthur ran to her, the woman who he had known all his life, rubbing his back against her legs, and enjoyed the feel of her hands as she rubbed his coat, running her fingers through it. He could hear the warmth in her words, even if some of them made no sense to him.

A hand went out above him, it held onto something that excited him, it was his favorite, a red ball, all covered with his bite marks, but it was his. The lady threw the ball as hard as she could, and out he would run, away to get it, but not too far, not from her. He grabbed the ball, rolled it around in his mouth, bounced around again, to show how clever he was to the most wonderful person he ever knew. Then once again he chased as fast as he could, back to her, to drop it to her feet, that she might do it again.

This time she threw it into the stream, a clear stretch of shallow water, as it trickled along over the shining little pebbles and rocks. In Arthur ran, splashing around, hearing her laughter, feeling the love she had for him, and together they would have so much fun. He nudged the ball, stuck under the water, before plunging himself into its icy coldness, grabbing it once again, holding onto it, shaking the water off and running, splashing back to her, so full of life, because she loved it and she wanted it, and she, she was all that mattered.

Days like this were often and wonderful, with the long walk back home, often holding the hand of her man, but not always, because sometimes he would be too slow, too much in pain to be there. Still, Arthur knew he loved him, and wanted to be there.

Sometimes the sun would not be so strong and joyous, sometimes it would be so cold outside that the skies were white and the ground crunchy to walk on. This lady, the sole center of his life, she would walk with him no matter how it was.

Now he was walking in the snow, struggling to see above it, it was so deep. When he breathed out, white whispers of vapor would come out, and she would laugh at him, calling him the doggy factory, whatever that was. She stopped and rolled up a ball of snow, but instead of throwing it for him to go and fetch, she lifted it into the air. He jumped as high as he could manage, because he was so clever, and she needed to know that. Arthur grabbed the ball in his mouth, as it disintegrated into an overflow of soft powder and freezing cold water. He licked at it, lapping away, spooning drifts of it to the floor. It was cold in his mouth, but so much fun that he ran to her, and away again. The lady picked up another rolled ball of the soft white stuff, throwing it even higher in the air, so that when it crashed down to him, it splattered around his mouth, covering him in snow.

The lady laughed so much, so hard, to see his whole head all white, as he stood there, open-mouthed, panting away, looking like part snowman, part dog. Arthur barked at her, he was enjoying it so much, in the perfect moment.

Together they walked on, into the fields where they always did, to the frozen stream. She didn't laugh so much then, as she stood looking into it. Tears seemed to be falling from her face, in a way he had never seen before. Without even seeing it, he could tell she was unhappy.

Arthur sat, in the snow, looking at her, as she looked back at him, with such sad eyes. He never saw her hold hands again with the man, in fact never saw him again, but every now and then he would notice his smell, on something she would hold.

Her face drifted off into darkness, as the cold of the snow gave way to the warmth around him, as once again he was back, laying under the bed, safe and sound, hidden.

CHAPTER EIGHT

It had been a long night, and Arthur was stiff. He woke to the smell of something amazing, a fine aroma, fish, food, bacon, bread, sauce, all those stinky but lovely things that all dogs, and most people love. He would have to see if the coast was clear, and if it was, time to go hunting.

Ever so slowly Arthur crawled away from his spot, front paws grabbing at anything they could, pulling himself ahead just a little. He stopped, peeking out from the edge of the bed, listening. He tried to see if there were any other smells, such as people, but of course no chance, because all his nose was telling him was that there was bacon - *go get it, why was he waiting?*

Finally plucking up the courage, he lifted himself from under the bed, just enough to see properly. All the while listening, padding forward just a little, wary of being discovered, at least before he could fill his tummy with it all.

There was no one home. He had slept that long. Light shone in through the windows, bright and clear. The house was empty, his toy cupboard, ready for a little dog to have some fun. He walked out onto the landing area, looked around, wondering where to go first. Would it be the toilet bowl for a nice drink from the hopefully cool crisp water, or would it be down to the kitchen for a banquet? As nice as the water seemed, food always came first. That was his unwritten rule, water or food, food first, sleep or food, food first, fun or food, well, you get the idea.

Casually as he could, Arthur walked down the stairs, feeling his mouth moisten at the prospect of all that was to come. He walked along the hall into the kitchen, looking up at the table, sniffing the air. He could tell there was food, exposed, just sat there, waiting for him.

The kitchen appeared all bright and welcoming, calling to him, with its fine scent. It wafted around teasing him, as if the food danced before him, wanting to be eaten. Arthur could take no more of it, sniffing rigorously, his nose raised up, prodding at the invisible scent. Over on the table smelt fine, but on the worktop counter, higher up, it seemed there were even more goodies. He stood, wondering which to go for, the easier, lower table, or the more delectable but higher up plates. Tough choice for a little doggy.

In the end, greed got the better of him, and he wanted the most and the best. Arthur walked over to the kitchen counter, a great long thick piece of flat surface, above it from closed cupboards, each offering temptation as to what they might hold for him. He wouldn't waste time trying to get in, he was far too lazy a hound to bother with that.

Arthur jumped up onto his hind legs, placed two front paws as best he could on the front of the counter and peered over. He could see three plates, each with a good portion of half-eaten food on it. Behind lay two bowls, spoons sticking out, covered in white sticky stuff, smelling as sweet as anything he had ever encountered. He wanted it, all of it, now!

Arthur tried leaning forward, using his tongue to lick at thin air, as he tried in vain to get at the food while standing on the floor. It was just out of reach. He thought about nibbling at the edge of the plate and pulling it towards himself, but he was just too short.

Desperation set in, as he jumped, a small amount, almost hopping on his two back legs. Being a mildly fat dog he was hardly one to jump around for joy any longer, even when he succeeded in getting at the food treasure. Any thoughts of acrobatics on the worktop were merely a foolish dream. Still, a greedy and hungry dog will never give up.

In a fit of temper, most unlike him, Arthur dropped to the floor, backed off, and ran at the counter, sprinting. Ready to go for it, just at the right moment he jumped, but too late as his head crunched into the front of the counter, nose squashed, mouth twisted as he slid into it full force, spinning around on the floor like a furry football.

It hadn't gone too well, but no matter, he was a determined doggy, and no food would ever evade him, he would get there one way or another. He walked this time, back to the worktop, and once again jumped up. Again he placed two front paws onto its edge, and looked over. Now pure strength would win the day, he would lift himself up by sheer force, and the prize would be his. Arthur pressed his small claws into the worktop, or so he thought. Pressing with all this might he lifted himself up, until his back legs were flailing around on the floor, waving around like a puppy paddling in nonexistent water. He held on for dear life, as if he were on top of a food mountain and falling might mean landing in a puddle of nothing.

He truly looked a sight, gripping onto the edge of the counter, looking forlornly at the food, imagining its taste any moment, legs flapping around like a hairy fish out of water. One last grasp, one last go and he would be... so he thought, until his front paws slipped both at once, and he fell, backwards, rolling around on the floor like a fool. He quickly dragged himself back to his feet, spinning around, out of breath, tongue out panting. He looked around, not for food for the moment, but to see if anyone was watching him make a pickle of himself. He was pleased nobody saw it. If no one saw it, then it didn't happen. There was nothing worse than being laughed at, especially since the time when he laid in bright blue paint on the floor and every time he walked past someone they pointed at him and laughed. He still didn't know what all the fuss was.

His attention turned to the kitchen table, round, not too high, but surrounded by smaller things which he might well succeed with. The chairs had been left underneath the table, all except one, where Billy was late for school and his mother had called him, loudly. He had run out, leaving the chair sticking away from the others, a gap, but perhaps one not too far.

Arthur jumped onto the chair, pleased with himself that he could see light at the end of the tunnel, a way to paradise. It was made of pine wood, and shiny, about half the height of the table. He stood on the chair, struggling to make all four paws work properly with it, but he was determined, as always. He dipped a little, lowering himself, then back up, then down a little again, preparing to jump. He was smart enough to know that if he got it wrong then the chair would slide back and he would never get another chance. It was all or nothing. Arthur had measured it up in his small mind, his instincts perfectly ready, as he finally jumped, leaping once again into the air.

He landed on the table, all four paws, to the slippery pine surface, sliding towards the edge. As he slid, all of the plates slid with him, one by one dropping off the edge, onto the floor, crash, crash, crash. Noise erupted, shattering around him, making him panic. He would either fall off, into a litter of food, and maybe hurt himself or he could do something. Arthur did something, twisting quickly, jumping once again without even thinking. He leaped, like a stallion lunging across a river, but furry instead and smaller. In an act of sheer bravery, and foolishness, he jumped from table to counter, landing perfectly, in the best fashion he ever had in his life.

Stopping dead, he wavered a little this way and that, head prodding against the wall cupboards, not daring to look around for fear of falling off, but he knew he had made it, he was where he wanted to be, that there wasn't a moment to lose. The food was calling his name.

So slowly, but not so that he looked like a ballerina ornament twisting in a jewelry box, but a purposeful dog, as if everything he did was planned, and not at all blind luck. The first of the plates was sat directly underneath him, touching one of his paws. It had a fish smell to it, with a few chips nearby, something which he very much loved. He had often walked past shops with such amazing smells coming from them, and his finest meals were from paper where some had eaten a little and thrown them into the bin, or even better, on the floor. An easy, tasty meal.

Arthur lowered his head gently, ready to taste perfection, then opened his mouth, taking the entire piece of fish in one go, one bite, one swallow and it was done. Then the chips, then the plate, licking it over and over until it didn't need washing any more, it could just go straight back into the cupboard for the people to use. He was so kind, so useful. Who needed a dishwasher when you had a dog, lick, clean, put away, done. How wonderful.

The next plate was even better, whoever it had belonged to (Abigail) had hardly eaten any of it. It had peas, chips, sauce, fish, even a full slice of bread, as if someone had put it there just for him. He gobbled it all up, like a hungry elephant trying to eat all the food on it before someone else came along and beat him to it. The more he ate, the more he wanted, the more he drooled for, well, more.

Once again he licked the plate, then just in case went back and licked the already spotless plate even cleaner. Yum.

There was one more, but it had very little on it, some big hungry man had eaten it, after he had washed all the dust off from a dirty cellar.

Arthur licked all three plates, once, then again, then, suddenly realized there were dishes, two of them with sticky white stuff, all that sugar, and who needed teeth anyway? He licked at them, unable to grab a mouthful because it was just too soft. He lapped away, every now and then swallowing, feeling the sweetness going down into his already full tummy, without a single care whether any more would fit. Too bad if it didn't, it was going in anyway!

Finally, he let out a large but not so nice burp, long and loud, proudly proclaiming to the empty home that he was full. Then he caught sight of plates on the floor, and his mind began to ask questions. Could he even get back down? He was so full, it wasn't certain. Could he even eat any more food? He began asking his stomach to move things along a little, quickly. No matter, he would just go for it, and see what came of it. Arthur lowered his front down, so that his front paws now hung over the edge of the counter, lowering himself, as if he could slide off the tiny drop. He did so, dropping, just a little, before falling off like a sack of potatoes, slapping onto the floor. It hurt, it wasn't great, but still, he was there. Right in front of him were bits of plate, with food all around it. No time to waste, he just began more eating, and more, and more, until his stomach pleaded with him to stop. So finally, he did.

It had been an amazing morning. He had slept so well, and now eaten a feast, and it still wasn't even half over yet. He was in a good mood, but needed to work off some of his weight. He walked out to the hallway, looking to the stairs. He could run around, like a mad fool, up and down the stairs, but he wasn't quite there yet. Instead, he would wander a bit, see what took his fancy, and who knew, perhaps another sleep.

Not yet.

He was too full to just lay down, he would burst if he did. Arthur wandered into the games room, looking around. Still it was filled with plush teddies of all shapes and sizes, strewn all over the floor. If the teddies had come to life and were bouncing all over it couldn't have been any better, so wonderful was it.

Arthur bounced, as best he could with such a fat belly, attacking the white teddy again. It looked at him as if it just wanted to play, apart from already being in pieces. Arthur dropped his front paws down again, as if to attack, staring at it, wide-eyed, clear in what he intended. The teddy was taunting him, it wanted to play, and he would, leaping at it, grabbing at it. He dragged it, this way and that, to one corner of the room, then the next, bounding along, occasionally nearly tripping. That was it, he would go for it, as he ran, holding onto the teddy with all his might, he dragged it quickly, lunging out of the room into the hall, into the kitchen, scattering bits of plate with it, then back into the hall, up the stairs, dragging along, rushing around like a crazy teddy and doggy act. It was mad but fun.

Down the stairs he hurtled, along the hall, back into the room. He dropped mister white teddy, dropped again, front paws lowered to the ground, looking at it, then yapped, once then twice, yap, yap, yap.

That was enough. Arthur panted heavily, his stomach was so full. The day had been rounded off perfectly; sleep, food, play, then more sleep. He drew in a deep breath, sighed ever so heavily, then slumped to the ground. His eyes glazed over quickly, as the warmth and comfort of the teddy room filled him with happiness. It was something he could get used to. Sleep washed over him, like a warm sea tide washing relentlessly in. He didn't mind, it felt so nice, as he settled down on his side, head dropping down. Still breathless, he opened his mouth, panting away. As he closed his eyes and sleep called to him, his long wet tongue flopped onto the carpet, a portly little doggy went fast asleep.

While he snored and dreamt of other things, the back door opened quietly. Arthur, without a care in the world, was totally oblivious to Abigail coming in for her lunch again. She closed the door heading upstairs, ready to get her sandwiches, before enjoying them in her favorite place outside of her bedroom: the games room.

CHAPTER NINE

Sleep. It was so lovely, like eating a plate of meat and not being full afterward, so you could do it all over again, and again, endlessly.

Arthur had slumbered down so intensely, feeling so comfortable, he had rolled without knowing onto his back. His tail was flopped out behind him and his legs poked up into the air. His mouth hung idly open, as if he were staring at something funny on the cream ceiling and laughing at it. In reality, his eyes were tightly closed, his mind filled with memories long past.

Abigail wandered in her usual daily routine up the stairs, annoyed by the chore of having to walk anywhere. She traipsed across the hallway, into the kitchen, opened the fridge and pulled a face at the sight that greeted her. Stuck in the middle of the fridge was a white plate, adorning the top of which sat four perfectly formed sandwiches. They looked thin, as if the contents were so thin that taste would be more of a past memory of how it should be, rather than how it was going to be. Beside the plate was a packet of crisps, one of her mother's pet things, putting crisps in the fridge, much like ironing socks and towels, an oddment shared by few.

Still, it was enough. Abigail took the plate out, avoiding the crisps, fattening and all that. Closing the door she looked sideways to get a beaker for her drink, only to finally notice the mess again on the floor. She looked at it ponderously, her mind absent of any particular interest, other than to note someone wasn't going to be happy.

Abigail filled the beaker with juice from the fridge door dispenser and turned, robot style, heading to sit and eat. She got to the games room door, then stopped suddenly, glad she had remembered before she was sat down that her most precious possession was out there calling to her. Quickly she rushed to it, as if it might disappear, into the lounge, to the coffee table, there it was, in all its shining glory: her mobile phone.

It needed dexterity to manage, but she could do it, years of practice. First, she placed the plate on the table, then took the phone, dropped it into her skirt pocket, then picking up the plate again she meandered back out, heading to the games room. Though forbidden by Mother from eating anywhere but the kitchen, when she was home alone she ate where she pleased. The lounge was simple enough but she loved the games room, so relaxing.

If she could have put the drink or plate into her pocket and kept her mobile telephone in her hand she would have, so urgent was her need to check out her social media, and see which of the best looking and nicest boys had commented on her posts. She rushed through, made her way through the scattered piles of teddies and sat smack bang in the middle of the floor. There were bean chairs around, but the floor was soft and welcoming and made her feel grounded, connected to her home in a way she had lost touch with lately.

Abigail sat easily down, perfectly balancing her drink and plate, setting them both on the carpet in front of herself. Without another second she grabbed her phone from her pocket, held it in one hand, switched it on, fired up Instagram and began flicking through. Her other hand reached out for her plate, fumbling around for a sandwich. As determined as she was to eat, she was equally determined not to take her gaze off the screen, for fear of missing something. Every now and then she stopped everything, pouted, clicked a photo to upload and once again continued fumbling.

Finally, she took hold of something edible and shoved it in her mouth, without blinking.

She remained completely oblivious to a particularly odd-looking teddy laid next to her, its legs pointing skywards, its mouth wide open, tongue hanging by its side, as it dreamt about love and other things.

Arthur was having a whale of a time, such was the comfort of his surroundings, and the softness of the carpet. This time though was different, but he couldn't quite put his paw on it. He felt close to something special, more loving than he was used to or had felt for a long time.

Dreams ended spectacularly as he opened his eyes and looked around without moving. He was in no mood to move much, because for the moment he was too comfy to do so, and besides, he was mindful to drift back off to sleep, soon. Something seemed different, but he couldn't immediately tell what it was.

"What, no," a voice beside him proclaimed loudly. That feeling of comfort evaporated as a deep sense of dread set into his stomach. He knew someone was nearby, possibly looking at him in horror, but he couldn't pluck up the courage to actually look. He could hear something or someone eating, munching away on food. His first instincts were to turn over and wait for his little bit of it, because of course everyone always saved him a bit. Sense took over, and he realized that if he were spotted, there would be more than shouting.

Arthur tried his best to see from the corner of his eye what was going on. He could just make out the young girl, sat a mere foot away from him, stuffing food into her mouth, her gaze fixed tightly on a small bright screen.

"No way," she said again, louder this time, in between nibbling on her food. He wondered if perhaps she wasn't aware he was in the room after all, much like he was, too engrossed in food to notice much else. Little did he know her real interest was online.

Everything froze as Abigail stopped, lowered her phone, ceased eating and looked around. Arthur continued to lay on his back, legs in the air, only now his mouth was closed. He struggled to keep it closed as his chops were so floppy the sides of his mouth kept spilling open, and his tongue appeared determined to flop out at every opportunity. For now, he was safe, just.

Abigail looked around, into the room before her gaze settled on Arthur. He returned her look, peering at her as if any moment she would scream and run around like a terrified chicken. As much as she stared at him, her eyes failed to focus, as his remained locked on hers, waiting, barely daring to breathe.

"No chance," she said to herself, before once again looking back at her phone. She dropped the half-eaten sandwich onto the plate and began flicking her screen.

"Oh no," Abigail shouted, suddenly jumping up to her feet. It was all over, as Arthur panicked, he twisted round, landing on all fours, still crouched. He would have to run, to hide, but where, she had seen him, out of the door, but then where? The cellar wasn't nice, and if she knew he was there, she would chase him, and call for others. He was in trouble and he knew it.

Without another word Abigail left everything and ran out. She headed straight down the hall, down the stairs and out, muttering *I'm late for school* to herself. Arthur just waited, and watched, ready to snap, jump up and run if need be. Perhaps she had gone for help, perhaps she had panicked herself and was hiding. He decided the best thing would be to run, anywhere, to hide himself. The moment he stood up, his attention was distracted by the plate of food. As much as the phone called to the young girl, so the food called to him. He gazed at it, his head unmoving, his eyes looking up and around but always back to the sandwiches, half-eaten and begging to him.

Any concerns he had about being caught were washed away as he gave in to temptation. He opened wide and nabbed a sandwich whole, before gulping down the half-eaten second one. Finally, he licked the plate, making sure not to leave even a single crumb. For good measure he let out a large burp, acknowledging that he had eaten a great deal today, and for that reason it had been just fine.

There would be no further running, as his belly hung down, reminding him that he had eaten, and eaten and eaten, until he was fit for bursting. He looked around, spotted a useful plant and walked over to it, before lifting his leg and beginning to do what he needed to do for some time, have a wee.

Arthur wandered out, looked around to see if any more panicking people were coming for him, and when it was obvious no one was he made his way back up the stairs. It had been fun, but there was nothing quite so safe and comfortable as his little space under the bed.

Slowly he crawled, dragging his round belly along the carpet, underneath, into the darkness, and flopped down, too full and fat to do anything else. Once again sleep took over him.

CHAPTER TEN

That lady's face, the one he knew oh so well but now only in his dreams. Now that face was cheerful, images of sadness long gone, but she looked different. Her hair was white, her face held a few more lines, but her eyes were still that vibrant blue, and her smile was always so welcoming. As Arthur lay dreaming, his mind filled up with images of her, flashing to moments of shared joy.

Now they were in a garden, one much like the one of the house he was in now. It had a fine lawn in the middle, with dug out borders all around, and rose bushes spread out across. Each bush was adorned with full colorful flowers, some bright red, some luscious pink, others sparkling yellow. The smell of them filled his nostrils and he would often sit in the middle of the garden allowing their scent to waft around him.

The lady, so quiet and yet gentle often knelt on something, small trowel in hand, digging out weeds, pottering away to herself, and for too long alone doing so. She seemed happy enough, but if he thought she needed some affection he would sidle up to her, nudge her and together they would hug.

Now she stopped a moment, sitting uneasily, leaning sideways a little, rubbing her wrist. She looked uncomfortable, and Arthur wondered if it was hug time. She looked at him with a pained expression as she rubbed her hand, but still, the old energy was still there.

Arthur quickly stood up and ran to a toy, a worn cuddly toy with its tail missing. He leaped on it, grabbed hold of it with his mouth and shook it quickly, as if he were in the battle for his life.

The lady laughed, clearly cheered by his madness. He jumped up with it in his mouth and ran, first to one corner of the garden, down low, then back up and to the other end. Each time he shook the toy, as if he were shaking it to pieces, but always with one eye on her, making sure he had her attention, that she was enjoying it, and feeling as happy as he did.

Now she clapped and smiled, and Arthur ran again, spinning around in a circle, before bounding over to her, dropping the toy. The lady picked it up and made to throw it. It didn't go very far, but it was enough, wonderful that she was joining in his fun. Again he grabbed at it, ran to her and dropped it, and again she laughed with him. Arthur panted, alive from his exertions, saliva all over the toy, but it didn't matter, she still threw it again, and again, and before long she too was out of breath.

Finally, she stood up, ready to go back in. She didn't walk as quickly as she used to, but Arthur did, and ran indoors, lapping quickly at his big bowl of water. The lady came in shortly after, sitting in her chair. She was quiet as always, and Arthur once again walked over, laying at her feet. Together they both slept, soundlessly, so quiet nothing could be heard.

CHAPTER ELEVEN

"What's this?" a voice shouted, louder than he had ever heard, at least since he entered the house. It was the second time someone had shouted and woken him, neither time being pleasant. Arthur lifted his head abruptly, banging it against the underside of the bed. Thankfully for him, it was soft, but still he felt the need to go. He scrambled out, sprinting out onto the landing, forgetting about the possibility for a moment that someone could be stood there. Luckily for him, no one was.

"I don't believe it," the voice came again. The shout was from Nancy, home early. Banging noises echoed from below, as pots and plates were scraped up from the kitchen and bins filled with debris.

The noise ceased for a moment. He wondered if it was all done and dusted, as he stood, listening. He was wrong, as feet stomped on the floor, heading up his way.

Arthur looked around quickly, frantic in his need to get away, anywhere. He ran, away from the sound of stomping feet, imagining he was being chased. The truth didn't matter in such circumstances, all that mattered was getting away, and hiding.

"Someone is going to bed early tonight," Nancy muttered under her breath as she stomped up the stairs.

Arthur ran straight into the bedroom ahead. It opened out, being the largest bedroom in the house. Flat against one wall was a large bed, the biggest he could ever recall seeing. For a moment he imagined jumping right on it and bouncing up and down, maybe messing up the perfectly formed covers, but the stomping feet put paid to that. There was a long wall of wardrobe doors, and in one corner a dressing table, none of which offered anything decent to hide in. He stood in the middle of the floor, looking ahead, then back, wandering around trying to see anywhere to go.

"I cannot believe that," a voice said right outside the door. Within a few seconds shouting and screaming would ensue, not to mention chasing. In the last second the woman stopped, walking into another room.

The bed, that was all there was, he would have to go for it. He charged ahead, straight at it, head down, intent on getting underneath it no matter what. The gap was dark, but not the same as the boy's bed, he didn't know if he could fit.

"I need a bath, no, a shower," the voice said again, talking to no one but herself.

It was too late to think about it, Arthur stuck his head under the gap, his whiskers telling him straight away that he had made a mistake, he could barely get his fat head under, let alone his fat body, or his fat bottom.

He barely had seconds, with his bottom sticking right up he could just imagine what it was going to feel like as the woman kicked him like a football.

He scratched at the thick carpet with his front paws, using his back legs to push with all his might. Slowly his head squeezed under, sliding along as his long, floppy ears pushed into his eyes. He scrambled hard, pushing with all his might. His body squeezed in, pressing down underneath the low bed, forcing air out of him, until finally only his bottom stuck out. Being the largest part of him, he doubted he was going to get it in, but getting out was going to be even harder.

He could hear the door slide open as the woman walked into the room. Unable to bear a kick he pushed with all his might until his bottom plopped under, and he dragged himself into the tight squeeze. Unlike the boy's room, there was nothing under there, except an odd dog. It was even clean, no dust, clearly the adults liked a clean room, which to him was one good thing, even if he was beginning to look like a furry pancake.

He lay there, breathless, not daring to pant. He was somewhat stuck, afraid of what she might do with him there. She might poke a broomstick under and hit him on the bottom. For now, he could be totally quiet.

The woman breathed out a long sigh, before dropping down onto the bed. She dropped with a crunch, flouncing on the soft mattress. Her feet stuck out of the side as Arthur looking directly at them. As she dropped, the bed sagged hard onto his face.

"Blah," Arthur went, giving out an uncontrollable gurgling sound as she sat. He had been squashed before, but now he was truly flattened.

Nancy pulled a face, looking around. "Don't tell me the mattress is going," she said quietly to herself.

She stood up a little, before dropping back down again.

"Blah," Arthur went again, as air pressed out of his body like a deflating balloon.

"It's going to be one of those days," Nancy said, quickly undressing. She walked out for the bathroom as Arthur laid, wondering if his head had taken a new shape. He couldn't move, having sagged onto his side, with the bed pressing down on him. He tried moving his legs in a walking fashion, but being on his side he simply looked like a cartoon character and got nowhere. It was going to be a struggle, but he couldn't stay there, if they both got into the bed he really would be flat.

Suddenly Nancy burst out singing as she went to the bathroom. It made a pleasant change to hear her being a little happier. He loved it when he could hear someone sing, it would remind him of the times past, which seemed so distant now he wondered if it were even real.

The sound of singing dulled a little, signifying that she was in another room. It was now or never to get out and hide somewhere safer. Arthur scratched and struggled, unable to get a hold of anything. He had slid sideways completely, his paws sticking right out, his head squashed by the soft underside of the bed. There was no other choice, he would have to do what he always did in tight situations: panic! He scrambled, tried to roll, scratched, shook himself, grunted like a pig, made like a horse galloping along, and achieved nothing.

An urge entered his mind, one that he knew wasn't going to go away. He had eaten a ton of food, more than was usual for a pooch such as he, used to the streets and grabbing bits and pieces, scraps here and there. It had to go somewhere, and soon.

Arthur laid, looking sideways at the world of the bedroom. He relaxed a moment, thinking how warm and safe it was under there, even if it was a bit squashed. He thought about all the days he had been out in the rain, wandering the streets, even in the snow, trying to find somewhere that wasn't so cold he was frozen to his core. Compared to that, where he was now seemed a pretty good thing.

As he relaxed he felt the bed ease off from his sides, and began to get the message that he could move after all, if he just didn't struggle so much and breathe so heavily. He used one front paw, slowly grasping at the carpet, and pulled. Surprisingly his body moved, so he used his other front paw and pulled with that too, and slowly but surely he edged forward. He looked like a canine snail, moving so slowly that he could hardly be seen.

Eventually, he popped out just enough to get a good grip, turn and stand so that he could drag his bottom out. He stood again, relieved that he was free from his sagging prison. Yet another close run thing. He was turning out to be quite lucky in his newfound home. Or so he thought.

He took in a deep breath, about to sneeze, when the sound of movement interrupted him.

"What, no towels? You've got to be kidding?" Nancy called. Arthur wondered for a moment if she were talking to him, but of course, she was talking to no one again.

Nancy barged into the room, completely naked, her hands in the air as if she were grasping for an invisible towel. Arthur looked at her, terrified that any moment she was going to react. Instead, she appeared to be frozen, eyes closed, looking at nothing, fumbling around for something that wasn't there. She edged forward, staggering, arms flailing, her face and hair covered in soapy wash. She couldn't see a thing.

Arthur leaped away, almost knocking her over, shooting out of the bedroom door.

"What, who's that?" Nancy asked, still fumbling around. She had felt something run across her legs, but was too distracted to deal with whatever it was.

"Ow, ow, ow that hurts, soap," she said, finally reaching the bed. She grabbed ahold of the bed covers, rubbing her face frantically.

Arthur disappeared out into the hall again, unsure of what to do. He finally realized the bed was a good place to be, but he had an urgent need for his daily thing, to go into the garden, to deal with all that food.

As he pondered, he caught sight of a naked woman exiting the bedroom. No time to lose, he went quickly into another room, one he hadn't yet seen before. As he entered, the place was full of steam, water running from a pipe on the wall. Everything was covered in wet mist, the floor soaking wet, as hot water smothered everything in mist.

Nancy suddenly entered, forcing Arthur to back up, until he felt his tail brush against the sink on the far end wall. Without even noticing the dog stood looking at her, she entered the shower, closing the glass door. She continued to wash herself, turning to face the wall, oblivious to what had occurred.

"No towels indeed, I'll use his t-shirts I will," Nancy muttered, too busy being angry to think about anything else. Arthur slowly walked ahead, trying to sneak past. As he did so Nancy opened the door a little, threw out a soaking wet flannel, hitting him squarely on the head, soaking him in the process.

Now two were angry, one over a messy kitchen, the other because It wasn't time for his yearly bath and yet here he was, soaked already.

He walked down the hall feeling sorry for himself. He was bursting to go to the toilet, was soaking wet, and constantly having to run away. He began to wonder just how good this new home life was. He had been well trained, and knew he couldn't just go anywhere he wanted, so would have to wait. Even if it meant he got caught, something would have to give.

Arthur wandered to the stairs and sat, wondering what to do. Was it over? Should he just go say hello, and see what happens? He had nothing left to do. He upped and walked over to the large bedroom, walked right in and sat once again at the end of the bed. He would wait, and then she could come in and they could get to know one another. Maybe.

Minutes passed, then more, until it became too tiring to sit. He slumped down, deciding a quick clean was in order. The last thing he needed was to be unclean when his new owner walked in. Besides that, he enjoyed licking his paws more than anything. It was his hobby, he could spend hours just making them wet and then drying them off, all with his super useful tongue. He could never understand why people didn't do it more, but they liked soap which was not good at all.

The light had begun to fade a little in the room, and the heating had kicked in. It was just so nice, like a giant, warm, room-sized basket to slumber in, and the carpet was particularly nice. Sleep beckoned. His introduction would have to wait.

Everything went dark, as a soaking wet t-shirt smothered him. Before he could react another hit him right on the head. He could see out of a gap between them Nancy picking shirts from drawers in the opposite side of the room, drying herself off and throwing them behind herself.

"That'll teach him not to use all the towels," she whispered to herself, laughing as she did. It was a light-hearted sentiment, one which she knew they would giggle over later. Once he had calmed down that was.

She pulled on a dressing gown hung from the back of the bedroom door and walked out. Arthur didn't know what to make of it, except the fact that yet again he hadn't been seen. He wondered if perhaps he wasn't really there after all. No matter, he had more cleaning to do, once he got away from the wet shirts. He upped and walked out, no longer so concerned about being caught.

CHAPTER TWELVE

"It wasn't me, it was her."

"No, it wasn't!"

"Yes it was, it wasn't me."

"I saw you do it."

"Muuum, waaaaaah."

"Enough, both of you, enough," Nancy shouted. It brought instant silence as both children looked directly at their mother.

"Billy, go and take your school coat off, take your shoes off, and go to your room until your tea is ready."

"But Mum, I..."

"Now."

Billy began to offer his loud, fake crying, that which he often used, mostly unsuccessfully. Even though it rarely ever worked, for some reason it made him feel better, so he carried on with it regardless.

"Abigail, the garden is full of leaves, you were supposed to do it ages ago, and now it's worse than ever, so you go do it, or no pocket money this week."

"But Mum, I..."

"Now."

Abigail turned quickly, as if the harder she turned the more impact it would have. Given the state of the kitchen and the mess their mother had had to deal with, nothing was going to work. It would be her way, or the highway, whatever that meant.

Billy got so far down the hall, dropped his coat onto the floor, kicked off his shoes and ran upstairs. His mood lasted all of four seconds, until an idea popped into this head that he could play with his toys, after which nothing else mattered.

Abigail went down to the lower floor, looked out at the wind sweeping piles of brown leaves around, and decided to play too. Only she would play at being awkward. She opened the back door, allowing gusts of cold wind to blow in. It wasn't nice out, but no matter, it could be the same indoors too.

She opened a door opposite, pulled out a large rake and a roll of sacks, then stepped out into the garden. It was the worst job in the world to her, but she needed her pocket money, life would be over without that.

The cool air wafted up into the house, lingering and drifting, until it caught the nose of a sleepy dog. It felt and seemed fresh, enticing, something he would enjoy, if only it were a little warmer out. Arthur stood up, weary and stiff, but so full he had no choice. He could hear voices, wondering who was where, and what any of them might say. He peeked his head out of the bedroom door, looking around for signs of trouble. He could hear Billy making odd noises in his room, but nothing else. He would risk it. Slowly he walked down the hall, past Billy's room; the door was pulled to, a little light spilling out from it, but otherwise OK for now. He continued, heading for the stairs, then down. Below was all light, as everywhere was lit up, including the hallway. He could hear the voice of someone singing, perhaps Nancy again, lowly, just to themselves, but it signified that she was distracted. He had his chance.

"Leaves glorious leaves," Abigail sang, kicking piles of leaves all over. She wouldn't enjoy cleaning it all away, but at least she could have some fun doing what she wasn't supposed to do.

Arthur peeked around the door, looking out at her. The air smelled cold but sweet, inviting to him. It was nice being warm indoors, but he was so used to the cold that it had become second nature. He watched Abigail kick around for a moment, wary not to frighten her by being seen. She seemed to be having so much fun, he could imagine rushing out and joining in, bouncing around the piles and rolling in them. It sparked memories of doing it before, when he was much younger. It was tempting.

He would do it, go for it, join in her fun. He leaped out of the house, to the small patio area and onto the grass. Abigail had her back to him, looking once again at her phone, gazing upon it as if it were a crystal ball.

Quickly he ran onto the grass, running round and round in a circle, looking for just the perfect spot. Every few seconds he looked at her, just to make sure she wasn't watching him. He enjoyed his privacy when going to the toilet; the last thing he would need was a young girl watching him squatting down.

It was a huge relief, as he waited, allowing nature to take its course. There was no rushing such a thing, he had to be sure he had done everything, most importantly so that he could free up some much-needed space to eat more!

Finally, he was done. For good measure, he quickly lifted his leg against the rake that Abigail had kindly left for him, and popped back into the house. It might be a nuisance trying to avoid being caught for him, but it was early tea time and he was feeling peckish again. He ran in, back up the stairs, then up the next, until he was stood on the top landing. Ahead he could see the light from Billy's room. His next challenge would be to get under his favorite bed with the boy there.

"Mum," Abigail shouted.

"Muuuuum," she shouted again.

Nobody replied. Her anger growing, Abigail leaned in through the door. She wasn't going to go up, her mother could come down to her.

"Muu..." she began to call, only for her mother to suddenly appear, walking down the stairs to her.

"What is all the fuss, Abi?" Nancy asked. She only ever called her by her shortened name when she was angry or tired. Today she was both.

"I'm not cleaning that up," Abigail said sternly. She was determined to give as good as she got.

"I did say if you don't clean up those leaves you will not be getting your pocket money."

"Not that. That!" Abigail said, pointing to a large pile in the center of the grass.

Nancy's eyes lit up at the sight of Arthur's huge deposit.

"Oh no," Nancy said, screwing her face, sickened by the sight.

"Exactly," Abigail said, shoving the rake at her mother. "Plus now the rake is wet on the bottom too, and it's not from wet leaves."

Nancy shook her head. "I bet that's from the neighbor's dog, he keeps getting in here. I guess that's another job for me," she said, shrugging her shoulders.

Abigail just looked at her mother, not wishing to join in the conversation, because there was no way she was going to help out.

The commotion from below triggered a thought in Arthur's mind, that any moment the boy would cotton on that something was going on and he would come running. Rather than wait and have to panic, he trotted ahead, finally turning into Abigail's room. It was the only room in the house that had no lights turned on, offering sufficient darkness to hide. He entered the doorway, turned and watched, hopefully.

Like clockwork Billy came running out, holding a toy soldier in his hand. Like clockwork he tripped at the top of the stairs and fell forwards, rolling and tumbling down the stairs. As he finally got to the bottom he stood up, made sure in a fraction of a second that nothing was wrong and then rushed off once again, tripped on the top of the next stairs, and rolled and tumbled down once again.

Abigail and Nancy looked back at the house, as Billy came rolling down the stairs and into the hall.

"Billy, are you alright?" Nancy asked. He stood up, looked around and nodded quickly.

"He does that on purpose," Abigail said, wishing she were somewhere else.

Nancy leaned over, pushing a shovel underneath the messy pile, watching it scrape along the grass. Billy laughed, pointing at her. It was a mess, after all, a mess of a day for her.

Quietly but quickly Arthur made his way to Billy's room. He was growing used to the family, quite enjoying their odd ways. The children were a handful, but fun. As he entered he saw a pile of papers and toys against the lower outside of the bed, blocking his way. Far from being cleared out underneath, Billy had somehow managed to stuff even more rubbish underneath. Still, it was his home, his bed, and he found a way in, using his front paws to drag things away. Again he lowered himself, using his paws to drag himself in until he was back in the corner, safe and secure.

Arthur began to lick his paws again, quietly cleaning off the mud from outside. It had been a good day so far, though a snack wouldn't be out of the question.

"I didn't poo in the garden," Billy said, trotting back up the stairs.

"I didn't say it was you that did it, stupid, I said..."

"Abi, do not call your brother stupid," Nancy shouted.

"But he is."

"Last chance, or you're grounded for a week."

"Right," Abigail said, huffing loudly. She barged past her brother, stormed up to her room and slammed the door.

"And don't slam your bedroom door either."

Abigail opened her door again, then slammed it louder. Billy slunk back into his room, deciding to stay out of it.

He had forgotten his toy soldier but felt annoyed, angry with himself. It was too much to go and find it, so he would have to do something else. He sat on his carpet, surrounded by toys. There were cars, plastic planes, a tub of odds and ends, and piles of boxed board games in the corner. Spaceships, he would play with spaceships, so began searching through papers and things, trying to find his favorite toy. He reached under the bed, groping around, trying to find where it was. He knew it had been there, he had been playing with it only days before.

Arthur pulled back, trying to get away, only to be blocked by the wall. He had felt settled, sure he could deal with them, that the mother might somehow welcome him, but he knew if the children saw him they would scream and run. He could see Billy's hand moving further in, mere inches away from him. He would love to be stroked, to feel the warmth of another as they hugged him, but it had been a long time since, and none had shown him any love for a long time.

"Gottit," Billy called, grabbing something and pulling away. He held up the toy, smiling to himself. Arthur was hidden in darkness, away in the corner, but he could see enough of what was going on. The look on the boy's face was fascinating, all joy and eagerness. He had long been interested in how children reacted to things, but rarely had they ever shown him any interest. He could imagine how much fun it would be to go running and playing with them, fetching and chasing a ball or something.

"Vroom," Billy said, waving his toy robot this way and that. He flicked a button on its side and wings popped out. Then he pressed another button and a light flashed as he zoomed it in and out, up and down all around. Arthur stared at him, wondrous at the look in Billy's eyes. The boy was lost in another world, truly enjoying himself, so happy. Something he had forgotten how to feel.

The play was interrupted with a knocking at the door. Billy looked over as it opened as Abigail poked her head around. As she did he figured she was going to shout at him to keep the noise down, or say something sarcastic about how childish he was. Sometimes she could be so mean.

"Hi," she said, quietly. It was unusually restrained from her, allowing him to be hopeful that this time she might be different.

"Hi," he said back.

"Can I come in?" she asked.

Billy hesitated for a moment, thinking to ask why, but then he thought how she had asked permission, rather than just barging in and shouting. As she was prepared to be different, he would at least try too.

"OK," he said, watching her intently.

Abigail entered, before pushing the door closed a little and sat down beside him. It was obvious she was in a quiet mood, as she bunched up her legs underneath herself, smiling awkwardly at him. Billy was waiting for her to do something, to say something not nice, but it never came.

"What you doing?" Abigail asked.

"Just playing, with my spaceman."

"Not playing with your soldiers?"

Billy shook his head. "I left it downstairs when I fell, and couldn't be bothered going for it."

"Shall I go get it?" Abigail asked.

Billy looked at her, surprised. "How come?" he asked after a while.

Abigail shrugged. "Nothing really, I just thought it would be nice to get on for a change. I'm sick of being angry."

It seemed that she was being honest with him, from her expression, she was being nice. He wasn't going to say anything to mess it up, so simply nodded, smiling.

Abigail jumped up, opened the door and left. He sat playing, but his mind had wandered elsewhere, wondering if she would even return. Minutes later she came quickly in, all smiles, and held out his soldier for him, waiting for him to take it. In the past he would have snatched it off her, saying something sarcastic, but it felt different, that she meant it, and needed it. For once he would love to have someone to play with, even if it was his sister.

Abigail sat down beside him again and smiled back at him, watching him as he took the soldier. It didn't take long before he brought the two toys together, and began a plan to integrate them into one big imagined battle plan.

"You could use this box, it could be their headquarters," Abigail said, holding out an old shoebox. Billy was lost again in his own little world of imagination. It was something she used to enjoy and readily share, but as time had gone on and she had grown, such things no longer held the same interest for her. She missed it, and simply sat, watching her little brother wrapped up in it all. For a few moments they would share it, and find a new type of connection they had never shared, until then.

All the while, Arthur lay, his head resting on an old slipper. His eyes twinkled in the lights beyond, but he didn't blink, just stared, enraptured by their play. Though only a dog to some, he was worldly and intelligent enough to be aware of human emotion. He could share their feelings and warmth for one another, as much as their negativity towards each other. It was a special moment, and although they had no idea he was there, he felt as if he were with them. It was magic to him, that shared bond they held, like one he had shared with another long ago.

It had been a lovely day, full of fun and excitement. Sleep called him and he drifted off again into doggy dreams.

CHAPTER THIRTEEN

His dreams drifted back again, to voices and faces he thought he had long forgotten. As much as he loved the things he dreamed of, when he was awake, it all eluded him. In the cold light of day, there was only what was happening now, but in his dreams he was loved and loving, and ached so much to be there. Darkness in his mind flittered away like sand on a blowy day, presenting him once again with something more to remember.

"I'll be fine," the lady said.

"You'll be much happier somewhere that can help you manage better."

"No, really, I'm fine here. It's my home and I'm happy to stay here."

The woman looked at the lady, holding a firm expression. She tried to convey the sense of being nice, but the opposition of the lady she spoke to didn't sit well. She had her ideas, and they didn't match those of the woman she spoke to.

"Really though," the woman continued. She was sat on the edge of the flowery sofa, clipboard in hand, papers sat atop. She was dressed smartly, in a tight skirt and white blouse, her hair pulled tightly back into a bun. She had the look of someone who meant business, but tried to suggest otherwise with everything she said.

"No thank you," the lady persisted.

"The prices are exceptional," the woman attempted to say.

"Thank you for calling, we'll see you out," the lady insisted now, standing quickly. She felt the effects of her age, trying to hold her back, but for now, with this visitor, she would not give her the satisfaction of showing it.

"We?" the woman asked.

The lady looked down. "Arthur and I. He and I will see you out."

The woman looked at Arthur, sat beside his great friend, the woman whose life revolved around him, and his her. The two looked back at the woman, both glaring. There was nothing more to be said, certainly not as far as Arthur was concerned.

Without bothering to share another look the woman stood, smiled briefly and walked out. She opened the front door for herself, made a half-hearted effort to look back and nodded, before walking out.

The lady closed the door, pulling her cardigan closed. She looked at Arthur and smiled. "There's plenty of life left in me yet, and I'm not going into one of those nursing homes, just so they can take all my money."

Arthur couldn't entirely understand everything she said, but he knew what she meant, and most importantly what she felt, for him. He knew it because he shared it all with her, and more.

"Come on, let's go sit down," the lady said. He knew that much, it was his second favorite pastime, after eating of course. The lady walked slowly, her feet dragging a little on the wooden floor. She turned into the lounge, as Arthur rushed past. He was too full of life and love to realize how he behaved, but she knew what he was like. The lady held for a moment onto the door frame, until he had passed, then carried on.

As she walked into the living room she looked out of the window, seeing all the flowers in bloom, the vibrant reds and yellows, the stunning purples and whites, all flowing in the gentle breeze. It was like nature's orchestra.

"OK, let's sit down for a moment. Not long and he'll be here, we both enjoy that when he comes don't we?" the lady asked. Arthur didn't know how to nod, but it didn't matter, because as she sat he leaned against her leg, slumping down and sliding onto the wooden floor. The lady laughed, thinking how funny he was. He was like a cartoon character around her sometimes.

She leaned over a little to him. "Are you a silly boy?" she asked, smiling so happily. He leaned back, lifting his head upside down which he often did, so unusual for a dog, and yet so endearing to her how he acted.

The love shared between them was unconditional. He provided her with such comfort and companionship, and she provided him with hugs and food. What more could there be needed?

The front door opened again loudly.

"Hello, hello," the lady said.

"Hellooooo," a voice called back.

The lady looked quickly at Arthur and smiled even more. "Oh, he's here, go and say hello."

Arthur didn't. He knew who it was, more from their smell than their voice, and liked them very much, but he wouldn't leave her side. He would never do that, never leave her.

CHAPTER FOURTEEN

It was cold. The light was no longer so warm and bright. Arthur opened his eyes to it, having slept so soundly he hadn't even moved. He felt stiff under the bed, wanting to crawl out and stretch.

The toys were put away and all was quiet. Daylight filtered in through the window, making it obvious he had slept a long time.

He looked out, listening, trying to see or hear anyone or anything. There was nothing, gone again, all about their merry lives, and here he was alone again. Arthur was never one to feel sorry for himself, so instead of thinking about it, he climbed out, stretched as he wanted to, and went off again in search of a new adventure.

At first, he walked out onto the landing area, then suddenly burst off to the stairs, leaping down them as fast as he could. The stairs were covered in thick carpet making it difficult to run on, but it didn't stop him. When he was in the mood, nothing would slow him. He ran down the first flight of stairs, stopped a moment to see if anyone was watching, to admire his craziness, but when there wasn't off he went again, down the next flight, crashing down as if he were half running half falling.

Arthur got to the bottom, panting heavily. He enjoyed a good run, and a good mad moment just as much. He looked out of the back door glass, seeing the white frost on the grass. It was a reminder of just how cold it had become, that only a week before he would have been out there, shivering. He walked over to gain a better view. The bushes at the sides had lost their leaves, all bare, naked and brown, except for a frosty coating, making them look like spindly white stalks pointing up to the sky as if in search of the sun.

The grass was perfectly even, a uniform blanket of ice, betraying the life beneath. As he breathed he noticed a slight flow of vapor coming from his mouth. If it was cold enough indoors to notice it, he could easily see how bad it must be outside. Clearly, winter was truly drawing in, and soon with it the onset of snow. The last thing he wanted was to be stuck like a cat, hiding inside a cardboard box, shivering so hard his bones rattled.

Such was his fleeting attention, and his desire to get away from any thoughts of cold, his mind once again shouted to him, one word, one idea: run!

Off he went, charging back up the stairs, along the hallway, into the kitchen forgetting how slippery the floor was. Too late he tried to stop, turning his body around, clawing at the floor, but sliding along nonetheless until he crashed right into the freezer door. The sound made a huge whump sound, but it didn't matter to him, he was having too much fun. He leaped up, turned to run, before noticing from the corner of his eye that the fridge had opened.

As he watched, it swung slowly wide, bright white light spilling out into the kitchen, looking like an oasis, offering all a vast Aladdin's cave of food and goodies. If a Genie had awarded him any one wish, it would have been just that.

Arthur's mouth dropped wide open, his eyes mirroring it, as his mind triggered the realization that that before him was a wall, a mighty wall, of food, in all its glory. He walked slowly over to it, fearful that his mind was playing tricks on him, but it wasn't, it was real. There were rows and rows of food, packets of cheese, tubs of salad and sauces, unopened packets of butter and bottles with jam. Right there, in the very center, lay the grand prize, something so amazing he could barely comprehend it, but his mouth could, drooling like a tap.

His eyes filled up with visions of a large, well-cooked turkey, sat in the center of the fridge, on a large oval plate. One side of it had been carved off, but most of it was still in place. No one had ever warned him that dogs shouldn't eat birds, because of the brittle bones, so all he could see and think was full mouth and full tum. Any suggestion of waiting to savor it longer ended as his belly demanded action. He jumped up at it, trying to nibble the outside of the feast, but he was too small. Stretching up on his hind legs, he pushed his mouth out to it, just... one... more... inch... but no, so instead he tried licking it, as the tip of his tongue just caught onto a slither of meat. The taste was small, but wonderful, a tangy greasy taste, but still so wonderful. It was just the push he needed, to remind him that come what may, it would be his, all of it.

Arthur began jumping, dropping back to the floor, then jumping again, little doggy jumps, like a puppy trying to get to its mother's milk. It was a brave effort, but still no prize, as each time he landed back in the same place, empty mouthed.

There was no other alternative, as he dropped to the floor, slowly retreating. He was no coward, he wouldn't give up, he had won bigger, more difficult battles. Finally, Arthur charged at the fridge, leaping up at the last moment, flying into the air. In his mind, he would grab the turkey, nimbly lift it away and land gracefully. That all happened, in his mind. In reality, he was too fat to jump anywhere near enough to get to it, and instead simply crashed into the lower shelves of the fridge. Everything rattled and shook, as bottles inside fell over and food fell to the floor.

He lay, half in the fridge, half out, looking up to the turkey, as if it mocked him, laughing at how rubbish he was at getting to it. *Fat dog, fat chance,* it was saying.

No way would he give up, with so much food at stake. Sure he could simply grab a packet of pies from a lower shelf, but then while he was filling his boots with that, all the while the turkey would be dancing and singing, making fun of him. He had too much pride to allow that to happen.

An idea struck him as he lay looking up, as one of his paws was sat on a white wire shelf. As he tried to stand up, his claw caught in the gaps, allowing him leverage to stand up. It was just the signal he needed, as he pushed hard against it, lifting himself right up. He placed his other front paw on the next shelf up, straining to pull himself higher. Then his back leg stood inside on the bottom of the fridge, until he was stood in it totally. Finally, he lifted another front paw, slowly climbing, edging up until he was within reach of the golden goose, or turkey as it really was.

Finally, he had conquered the mountain, reached his goal, as he stood looking at it. If dogs could smile, then Arthur would be doing just that, glibly smiling before the banquet. He lunged at his lunch, grabbing it into his mouth whole, holding onto it for dear life. It was only then that he realized how heavy it was, but no matter, he was strong, as he pulled with all his might. It slid, turkey, plate and all back towards him. He was a strong dog, but not that strong, and it overwhelmed him. He felt himself fall back, doggy, plate and turkey, all going in one direction, backwards.

A huge crash welcomed the beginning of the celebration, as the plate smashed into pieces on the floor. The turkey skidded away to the far corner of the kitchen, as Arthur panicked that his joyous meal was escaping, wings or no wings. As he fell back his hind legs kicked out, but no matter what, his eyes never left the prize as it scurried away. His legs kicked at the door hard, sending it closed until it thudded shut. Once again the prize of food was gone, leaving nothing but a broken plate and a round, well-cooked turkey sat alone in a corner. In one fell swoop, he had both lost his prize and gained a bigger one.

Arthur stood up, trotting quickly over to the meat, afraid that somehow it might up and escape again. He eyed it eagerly, but finally, after all his efforts, he could tuck in to a nice lunch, and enjoy himself without the worry about what was going to get in his way. He opened wide, and bit down onto the top of it, right into a prime piece of fine white meat. It tasted amazing, better than anything he could ever remember having. He chewed away, looking up and around at nothing in particular as he ate, enjoying the lovely chewy taste. It had been cooked to perfection, and he knew it.

He took another bite, then another, and another, chewing off all the easily accessible meat, nibbling away, gnawing at it until all of the precious white meat was gone, into his tummy. He burped, loudly, signifying his enjoyment of it. He was surprised at how quickly he had become full, but he shouldn't have been, given his other fine meals in recent times.

Being such a greedy dog, his full tummy was never a signal to stop. Life on the streets had taught him that not eating when full usually meant that it would soon be gone to another, and when gone, it could be days before anything else came along, so the message was, eat, eat, eat, until fit to burst. So he nibbled some more, tugging at what was left, and then some. Something stuck out of the side, a wing or a leg, he couldn't tell which and didn't much care for the difference as long as it was edible, and even if it wasn't. A piece broke away, just the right size for his mouth, as he shoved it in whole, chewing away, cracking and crunching on something snappy. It wasn't much like the other bits, the pure meat, this required a bit more effort, but no matter, it still tasted all greasy and just fine to him.

Crunch. Snap. Click it went. He chewed hard, trying hard to overcome the toughness of it. It was a bit much, but he would have it anyway. He swallowed, as half of it went down and the other half stuck in his mouth. Signals went out into his doggy brain that something wasn't right, as he could neither swallow or bring it back; it was stuck! Arthur tried chewing some more, before choking, then chewed some more and choking again. The main thing was it tasted good. He gave it one last push, swallowing as hard as he could. Still it wouldn't go down, as he heaved right up, straining himself as much as he could. He looked like a bodybuilder, shoving his chest up and out. Suddenly he coughed, choking some more, as bits of turkey and bone shot out from his mouth all over the kitchen floor. He breathed in deeply, enjoying the refreshing air.

It was a hard lesson he had learned about birds and bones, but being such a bonehead himself, he, of course, had learned nothing. Arthur looked around, noted the bits of turkey on the floor, mostly from him and went about licking it all up, quickly, before anyone else came in a beat him to it. Finally, he opened his mouth wide, took a hold of what was left of the turkey and walked out, heading back upstairs. It tasted too good to waste, so he would have to protect it, his precious feast. He strutted along, back to the top floor, into Billy's room, before lowering down and scrambling under the bed. He nudged it into place, right in the corner, in the darkness. It was perfect, his new home, and now his own stock of food for whenever he needed it. Bones and all.

His timing was perfect, as the door slammed open signifying Abigail's entrance. He pushed back further into the darkness, hiding against the wall, comforting himself with a lick here and there of the last bits of turkey. Most of it was bone, but he loved bones anyway, and what was the odd bit of choking if it tasted good.

He could hear the stomp of feet as the young girl walked up the stairs, then off down to the kitchen once again. He thought it an odd thing, her routine, doing the same thing every day. He was glad his life wasn't like hers, he had a choice of what he could do, good or bad.

"Not again!" a voice shouted, as Abigail spotted the mess in the kitchen. Pieces of broken plate littered the floor, but there was no sign of any turkey, and the fridge was closed. It was a mystery, that somehow the bird had indeed escaped. She couldn't help but let loose a chuckle, at the thought of a cooked turkey somehow escaping the fridge and running off, of course not forgetting to close the door behind itself on the way.

Arthur licked the turkey once again, a final way to say thanks, before drifting off again into a wonderful restless sleep. What there was of it.

"Not again!" a voice shouted, interrupting his sleep. It seemed as if he had only just closed his eyes, and for some odd reason Abigail had shouted the same thing out. Only this time it wasn't her, it was Nancy, home from work, seeing the floor, seeing bits of plate.

"Did you do this?" Nancy asked.

"No, Mum," Billy replied. He hadn't even managed to take off his coat when he heard his mother shout. As he stood in the doorway he could just feel all eyes on him, no matter what he said, he would be blamed, he always was.

"Well it's either that or we have a rat in here," Nancy said grimly.

"Or rats, lots of them," Billy said excitedly.

"I hate rats," Abigail shouted, running away up to her room. Billy laughed as she went.

"Billy, please take your coat off and go to your room. Wait 'til your father hears about this," Nancy said, picking up pieces of plate.

"But Mum."

"No Billy, seriously, did the turkey just up and run away, after closing the door on itself?"

Billy shrugged.

"You're eight years old now Billy, you're too old for this."

He knew he couldn't win, and turned away, walking slowly down the hall, allowing his coat to fall from his shoulders, dragging it along. Life wasn't fair, he always got the blame.

Billy wandered up the stairs, aware it was no use arguing. No matter what, they were older than him, bigger than him, and could shout louder. Dad had never been one to raise his voice, but if need be his mother could, and often did when she was tired or stressed.

He walked into his bedroom, flicked on the switch, and slumped to the floor. He couldn't much find the energy to do anything. His toys sat looking at him, his posters on his walls, Buzz Lightyear, and Spiderman, both looked down, waiting for the fun to begin, but he wasn't happy, and so for now he would just sit and think about what to do, without actually doing anything.

"Hello," Stan called as he came in from work. Nobody answered. "Well don't all come rushing, will you?" he continued.

Nancy finally walked out from the kitchen to meet him as he walked up the stairs. "Guess what?" she asked.

"Erm, you're pregnant?" Stan asked, chuckling to himself.

Nancy's eyes lit up. "No!" she said, harder than she had intended. The sharp response instantly deflated any look of happiness on Stan's face.

"No tea for tonight," Nancy said abruptly, walking off to the kitchen again without waiting for a reply.

"What?" Stan asked, following on, hurt by the thought.

"Someone has taken the turkey which I had cooked for tonight's tea," Nancy explained.

"Who?"

"Well..." Nancy replied, shrugging but giving him a look which suggested she imagined it wouldn't be too hard to guess.

"Rats?" Stan replied.

"I hate rats," Abigail shouted down, slamming her bedroom door.

"Billy," Nancy replied, trying to suppress her anger.

"Billy?" Stan asked pointedly, his face all that was needed to show how daft he thought the idea.

Nancy nodded.

"How could he eat all that?" Stan asked, wanting to laugh but knowing how she would react. They were alike, worked hard and ended up tired, and didn't need so much hassle after a long day working.

"I'll have a word with him," Stan said, not entirely believing anything so silly. He was a handful at times, but even he would never do anything so foolish. Nancy nodded, continuing to clean up.

"Billy," Stan called as he removed his coat heading into the lounge. It was all dark, a clear signal that all was not well. Whenever there was a problem everyone would go off and do their own thing, leaving it as if it were an empty house, something he never liked.

"Yeah," Billy called down.

"Here, mate, come down a moment," Stan called back.

"Do I have to?" Billy replied, not wanting one of *those* chats, which involved an arm around the shoulder and a friendly, loving word about the dos and don'ts in life. They tended to be boring.

"Come on Billy, just a minute while Mum sorts out tea."

"Ha," Nancy snorted.

Billy stomped down the stairs, mirroring how his sister did it. It was always her thing, except when she did it no one noticed or complained. He was never sure if that was a good thing or a bad thing, but did it anyway.

As Billy entered the lounge, his father was just pulling the curtains closed. He walked over and sat on the sofa, waiting for the big lecture.

Stan walked over, sat down beside him, put his arm around him, gave him that look, and so it began. Again.

As the two chatted Arthur had laid, enjoying the warmth, feeling his full tummy, but as much as he didn't want to move, he couldn't escape the need to have a drink. He panted a moment, exhausting hot air, before stopping, worried someone might hear him. He waited, held his breath, and out it came again, panting like a dragon breathing fire. It was all well and good being so full and warm, but he missed going to the toilet as he pleased, here, there and everywhere. He waited, hoping the need would go away, but of course it never did. There was no alternative, it would need a trip to the never-ending source of water, the bowl in the bathroom, that looked round, white and large, but best of all, full of water.

Arthur crept out, looking carefully out onto the landing. It was dark, no lights except for Abigail's room, but her door was closed, music blaring out, with only a thin slither of light to show she was even there.

Quickly he dashed across the landing, into the bathroom, feeling the distinctly colder air as he entered. In a way, it was welcome, not as bad as it might be outside, but still cooler than under the bed. The toilet seat was up, and the bowl once again full, clean fresh water. He lapped at it quietly, enjoying how fresh it tasted.

"So, come on now, you know you can tell me anything. Do you have any idea where the turkey is?" a voice came through, growing louder by the moment.

"I don't know, Dad," Billy pleaded. Stan wanted to believe him, but didn't believe for one moment it had been rats that had taken it.

"Come on, get your pajamas on, and then we can go down and get tea," Stan said, finally following his son up the stairs.

"OK," Billy said, sighing deeply.

The sounds of voices growing louder spooked Arthur, forcing him to stop drinking. He looked around, stood in the darkness of the bathroom, terrified that at any moment someone would walk in, lights would go on and he would be discovered. His doggy heart pounded, frantic for an answer.

He watched as first the boy walked past, head down, shoulders slumped, clearly unhappy, followed by his father. The two went into the bedroom, providing a moment of relief, as short as it was. Should he run? Should he climb into the bath and hide? Should he follow them and say hello? He had no idea what to do.

"Come on, lad, let's hurry up and go get some tea," Stan said, sitting down on Billy's bed. Billy smiled at him nodding, looking for pajamas in his drawers.

Stan looked around, seeing all the toys on the floor. As messy as it looked, from his own experiences he could tell it was how it should be. As much as Nancy complained about all the mess, all there was, was a land of fun and enjoyment. It was so colorful, though the Fimbles wallpaper would need changing, he was too old for it now.

As he looked around, something caught his attention, making him stop and think. Billy looked at him, wondering what was going on.

"What's that?" Stan asked.

"What's what?"

"That," Stan replied.

"That what?"

"That smell."

Billy sniffed the air, noticing something odd. "Dunno, maybe socks?" Billy asked hurrying into his pajamas.

"No, I don't think it's socks."

Billy shrugged. Stan stood up, sniffed the air again, and began looking around. "I think you need to tidy this room up."

Just as he was about to bend over to search under the bed, Abigail came out running. “It’s snowing!” she shouted.

Billy’s eyes lit up, as he chased out of the room after her. The pair ran downstairs as fast as they could. The excitement was too much, forcing Stan to follow them quickly. He had long considered himself too old to get worked up at such things, but their excitement was infectious.

“Don’t run, don’t trip,” Stan shouted, wondering whether he was calling to the children or to himself. He hastily followed, trying not to trip.

Down the stairs they all went, as Nancy walked out of the lounge to see what all the commotion was. The family headed straight down, opened the back door and out into the back garden.

“Wow, that looks amazing,” Billy said breathlessly.

“Yes, because I raked all the leaves up,” Abigail replied, sounding smug.

“I hope it carries on, so we can build a snowman,” Billy shouted.

“Calm down, you’ve not even had your tea yet,” Nancy insisted. The four of them stood looking up at the sky and the white covering. It was as if someone had taken a paintbrush and a pot of white paint, wiping away any signs of dirtiness and discolor.

As the family enjoyed their moment in the cold, Arthur was once again on the move. He had filled his belly with turkey and now filled himself with toilet water. Now all he knew he needed was to release it all again. He wondered about the plants in the games room, but felt sure he would get caught, and besides, he needed a sniff to see where his new territory was.

For now, it would have to wait. Nancy called once again, and the noise from the family grew immediately louder as they all began to return. Arthur turned and ran, back into the bedroom, crawling quickly under the bed, snuggling up tightly to the greasy, smelly turkey, or what was left of it. He wondered if perhaps another nibble, but was already bursting to go to the toilet, so held back.

"Wipe your feet, Billy," Nancy called as she made her way back to the kitchen. Stan followed, wondering if he could ask what was for tea, but afraid she might tell him to cook it.

Abigail was once again lost in her phone, texting frantically about the snow and fibbing about how she had hit her annoying brother with a snowball.

The family finally joined for tea, eating readymade meals with microwave chips, on lap tables in the lounge.

"This is nice," Stan said, trying to make light of the situation. Nancy ignored him.

"It's not turkey though is it?" Abigail replied, tugging with her fork on the rubbery chips.

"Well, someone took it, and I'd like to know who did," Nancy said, not bothering to look up.

"Wasn't me," Billy said, trying to force half of his meal into his mouth in one go, so that he could escape into the snow-filled garden.

"Billy, slow down, you'll give yourself indigestion," Nancy said, pointing to him with her fork. Billy responded with a loud burp, looking at her as if to wonder what the problem was. Before she could say another word he stuffed the rest of his meal in his mouth whole, picked up his tray and shuffled off the sofa, heading for the kitchen.

"Now don't you go heading back out, you'll catch a cold," Stan said, struggling with a particularly chewy meatball.

"Right, Mum," Billy shouted, oblivious to the fact that his father had called him, not his mother.

Without a care in the world, Billy headed straight down the stairs, opened the back door and ran straight out into the garden. The snow had become a blizzard, falling so heavy that any prints he left in the snow were immediately covered. Billy ran around the outside of the lawn, not wanting to spoil the inside; he had an idea for that and didn't want anything to affect that. He wanted to run and shout, but knew if his parents heard him they would bring him in and that would be that.

Arthur stood at the top of the highest stairs, looking down. His face and muzzle pressed down as he stared, and listened intently. He could hear sounds from the lounge below, and what appeared to be the boy having fun. As cautious as he wanted to be, Arthur couldn't resist the urge to go out, at the very least to relieve himself, as much as the need for fresh air. He loved the warmth and safety of the house, but part of him couldn't help but miss his life outside. It was a tough choice, and an odd one.

The air blowing up was cool and fresh, a constant reminder of the life he had lived, offering a kind of freedom to do as he pleased, but still it came at a cost. Unable to ignore the call any more he crept down the stairs, constantly on the lookout for trouble. Light filtered through from the lounge door and the kitchen, but everywhere else helpfully was dark. Feeling even bolder he continued, down again, until he stood on the last step, just able to peer out. He could hear Billy running and playing, enjoying himself so much. It was quite dark out, but the snow brought a vibrancy to everything, offering an illumination combined with the grace of winter which no other season could quite provide.

Feeling brave, Arthur walked slowly to the door and looked out. Billy was crouched over, pushing what appeared to be a large roll of snow around the edge. As he pushed as hard as he could, the snow underneath pushed back. Large lakes of white fell from the sky, flittering around haphazardly. The snow drifted around with each turn of wind, but as ice-filled as it was it wasn't so cold as to be unbearable.

Apart from the reflection of the snow, there were few lights, orange street lights from a distance, making it difficult to see. Arthur knew he had to take a chance, quickly jumping out of the back doorway, feeling the sudden chill of frost against his paws. From the far side of the garden, he could see the boy rolling his ball of snow, plumes of white chugging out as he breathed ever harder. As much effort as it was, it was clear he was having fun. Arthur wanted so much to join in, to roll around in the snow, to bite at it and run around in circles, but deep down he knew if he did, he would be outside, permanently, and on nights like this, that wouldn't do.

He wandered over to the corner nearest to the house, beside a small wooden shed. The doorway faced the house, with a small patio area leading to it. The roof was covered in a thick layer of snow, looking as if it would fall off any moment. Arthur tried to sniff around near the drain, checking for signs of food. As full as he was, more was always welcome. It was a habit he would never break, after so long on the streets.

"Billyyyyy, have you got the back door open?" a voice shouted. It was distant but loud, and clearly his mother. Billy looked quickly up, worried that he would be ordered in. He ran to the door, looked in, searching around, noticed no one about and stepped in, banging his feet to shake free the snow.

"No, Mum, I'm just looking out," Billy said quickly.

The second he had finished his fib, he ran back outside and began rolling another ball, quicker this time. Arthur watched the fun, as the boy pushed around in circles, growing it larger and larger.

"Billyyyyy, it's getting cold up here, where are you?" his mother called again.

Once again he dropped what he was doing, ran back to the door, stepped in and clicked his shoes to clear the snow. His hands were freezing, and he was beginning to shiver, but he was determined to finish.

"No, Mum, I'm not," he said, figuring he had enough time to finish before anyone could be bothered to go checking. He ran back out, continuing with his eager work. He placed both arms around the ball of snow and lifted, struggling to lift it on top of the other, larger piece.

Arthur peeked around the edge of the shed, unsure whether he was being seen or not. For the first time since he had hidden in the house, he was truly torn, over whether to run back out onto the streets where he belonged, or simply to carry on and enjoy it for what it was. His instincts told him to run, go be free and enjoy it again, but his body said no, look at all this snow!

Finally, Billy rolled a smaller ball, before lifting it above his head as best he could, placing it on top of the rest. He bent over, grabbed snow and packed it at the sides, shaping it as best he could. He stood back for a moment, looking at his craftwork. It would need a scarf and a hat, maybe some coal and a carrot, but for now it looked good. He figured once they saw it, his parents would be so happy with it that they wouldn't mind his little white lie about being outside, and would instead help him finish it off.

"Billy," a voice called, only now much closer. He ran to the house, jumped in and headed for the stairs. As he disappeared into the darkness of the house, Arthur could hear voices, low chatter, close but not too close. He chose his moment, ran out into the garden, looking eagerly for something to lift his leg onto. There was nothing in sight, only odd shapes covered in cold snow. He had no choice, and simply went for it.

"I thought we said don't go out," Stan said, leaning over, eye to eye with Billy. The pair were stood at the top of the stairs, outside of the games room.

"I didn't hear you say that," Billy replied.

"I said it," Nancy said, coming out of the lounge.

"I never heard you say that," Abigail said, following her.

"Er, yeah, I think we both said it," Stan replied.

"You didn't," Billy replied, feeling emboldened by his sister's stance.

Everyone looked confused.

"Well, it doesn't matter, because..." Nancy began to say.

"Come and look what I've built," Billy said, turning to leave again.

Arthur looked up at the tall white figure, felt satisfied with his choice, lifted his leg and began to relieve himself. It was bliss and long overdue. He stood as long as he dared, enjoying the moment of fresh air and lightening up.

The growing sound of voices came just as he was finished. Arthur leaped away, heading back to the corner between shed and house as the family came charging down the stairs. He stood once again, hiding in the gloomy darkness, watching as they all filtered out.

"Tadaaaa," Billy shouted, holding his hand out like a showman, pointing towards the snowman he had proudly built.

Everyone watched, as steam rose up from Arthur's deposit. The heat melted into its base. As Billy turned to look at it, all eyes on his creation, the snowman leaned a little, seemed to stop, before proceeding to crash sideways to the ground.

"Awwwww," Billy said, looking on in despair. Abigail burst into fits of laughter, putting her hand over her mouth as if to pretend not to.

Stan and Nancy looked at her, frowning, but it was too dark to make out, and she continued.

"It's better than you could make," Billy shouted, glaring at his sister.

"Oh sure, like a caterpillar laying on the floor." Abigail retorted, laughing again.

"No come on, we can all help rebuild him," Nancy said, taking Billy's arm and walking over. Stan followed reluctantly behind, aware that he was still in his slippers and without a coat. Abigail stood for a moment, wondering if she could just go back in and up to her room, but she knew she wouldn't get far before the dreaded call came.

As Abigail walked over to join the group, Arthur quietly slipped back to the door and headed in. As much as he enjoyed being the king of the park, he knew when it came to comfort there was nothing quite like a warm house and easy food. In the darkness he hid easily, slipping back up the stairs, reasonably satisfied with his night's work.

"OK, Abigail you grab that bit, and I'll lift up here," Nancy said.

"Er, why is there steam coming off it? Did you have a wee after you'd finished your little snow caterpillar?" Abigail asked, screwing her face up in annoyance.

"No!" Billy shouted.

"Plus it stinks," Abigail continued.

"Abi, that's enough," Nancy shouted back.

"Yes, enough, though it does stink," Stan said, beginning to shiver. He would welcome any excuse to go indoors. "Should we go in and finish this tomorrow, when it's lighter and, er, not so smelly?"

Abigail laughed again.

"I want to finish it now," Billy pleaded. Nancy looked at him, at the discolored snow then back to the others. "Right, it's late, it's cold and we can do it tomorrow," she insisted

Stan and Abigail glanced at each other, smiling briefly. It was a good idea. Nancy placed her arm around Billy, guiding him gently, nudging him against his resistance.

Billy seemed upset, his plans for fun dashed.

"Look, we can have half an hour on the Xbox, before bed, how's that?" Stan asked, looking at his son. Billy looked up, smiled as best he could and headed in.

In the darkness of the stairs, Arthur continued to traipse up, going back to where he knew he belonged. It had been a short day, after so much sleep, but he couldn't help feel it had been a long day with it. Sleep was calling once again, not to mention more turkey!

"The snow might be gone by tomorrow," Billy suggested. He was sat holding his games controller, oblivious to his character falling off the map and going splat. Abigail was sat on a giant teddy, watching in awe at how bad he was at the game.

Stan was sat awkwardly on a bean chair, watching the clock tick to thirty minutes so slowly he wondered if time had stopped.

"No love, it's supposed to be here for a while," Nancy said, trying to reassure him.

"But it might be gone by the time we get home from school," Billy continued.

"No chance of that, none at all," Abigail chimed in.

"How do you know, it might be," Billy pleaded, his face a picture of annoyance, one especially reserved for his sister.

"Er, because it's Saturday tomorrow, and there is no school."

Billy's eyes lit up, but his expression remained the same. He was elated to know there was no school, but regardless he still found his sister most annoying, even if she was right.

"Right," Billy said, sounding completely at odds with his expression.

As if he had a built-in alarm, right on the second of thirty minutes past Stan sat forward and looked at Billy. “OK, that's it, time for bed,” he said brightly.

“Oh nooo, not yet, five more minutes,” Billy pleaded.

“Come on, early to bed, early to rise for the snow tomorrow,” Stan said. He had expected the complaints, and was ready for his response, but Billy was just as ready for his.

“Alright, I'll get up really early then,” he said.

“Sounds good,” Stan replied, beaming at his son's positivity.

“And I'll wake you up at the same time, to come and help me build it!” Billy shouted, jumping up and down.

Nancy laughed as the smile disappeared from Stan's face. “I could see that one coming,” she said.

“I didn't,” Stan replied, looking at his son, wondering where he got his ideas from.

“Bed,” Stan said, trying not to sound unhappy, but it didn't matter, Billy's plans were set and nothing was going to upset him. He ran to Stan and Nancy in turn, hugging them both, before running off up the stairs before anyone could say anything.

He charged into his room, breaking the perfect sleep Arthur had been enjoying. He was partly curled up around the turkey, dreaming about it. Billy jumped into his bed, and pulled up the covers, ready to dream about flying with snowmen and building huge igloos to live in.

Arthur laid listening to the boy settle, thinking about joining in his journey to sleep. He very much liked sleep.

Billy curled up, pulling his covers over his head, feeling settled, allowing himself to drift off, happy with his life.

Crack.

The abrupt noise brought him back awake again. He lay for a moment, wondering if it had just imagined it. He waited, then a bit longer, and nothing. Sleep called again, so he closed his eyes and settled down once again.

Crack.

The noise came again, a little louder. Far from sitting up and putting his light on, Billy pulled his covers closer, wondering what might be moving around his room, if something were breaking his toys or perhaps something was tapping on his window. He was too afraid to look.

Crunch.

It sounded like a bowl of cereal being eaten, before dying out.

Billy wondered if he should shout for help, to call for his mum, but decided not to, he couldn't bear the thought of Abigail making fun of him.

Something hit his window, making him jump. He had to look, and as he did another gust brought heavy spatters of hail and snow onto the glass. It brought a sense of relief with it, that maybe there was nothing in there with him, instead it was just more snow. The idea of that was good for him, as he pictured in his mind snow drifts outside so big he would be covered in it standing up. With that in mind, he closed his eyes, curled up even tighter, and drifted off again.

Arthur licked his paws, having enjoyed a bone. He had realized how tricky they were to eat, but it was too much to resist, he just had to. For now, he would fall back to sleep, endless comfortable warm sleep.

Together the boy and the dog under his bed drifted off into the land of nod.

CHAPTER FIFTEEN

Life was good, at least for a short time for Arthur. Maybe it wasn't so short, but since then it had seemed so, as the struggle on the streets stretched out into cold nights and hungry days alone.

Before then he had known kindness, as his mind drifted in sleep to the old lady, her smile so welcoming, so loving. She sat now by the open fire, her knitting fallen aside as she expected the man to come in. She smiled so much, so happy when he visited, overjoyed by his presence. It wasn't the man she knew before, the one that she and Arthur walked with, he never came back, but this one did, all the time.

The man walked in and Arthur lifted his head, his tail wagging away so quickly it was a blur. He always enjoyed seeing the young man, who would often throw a ball for him and feed him. Today was no different, as he walked over and hugged the old lady, and patted Arthur on the side. Then he went into the kitchen and grabbed a double bowl. He filled one part with water, the other with kibble, and placed it down on the floor near Arthur's bed.
"It's nice and warm in here, Mum," the man said. It was, so warm like always, how she liked it.

CHAPTER SIXTEEN

Billy opened his eyes suddenly. It was bright white in his room and colder than usual, a sure sign of something big going on outside. Normally he would open his eyes, dread having to leave his warm bed, and spend ages trying to find excuses for not getting up. When it was Christmas, his birthday, or it snowed, it was time for action.

Throwing off his bed covers he jumped up, leaped off the bed and over to the window. It was like a scene from a Christmas card, everything covered in thick layers of snow. He stood looking at it, imagining he was flying over the rooftops, like a bird, swooping down and back up again. The thought didn't last, as ideas of snowball fights, building bigger snowmen and sledding took its place.

He ran from his room shouting and hollering, straight into his parent's room. "Mum, Dad, it's been snowing," he shouted, jumping onto the bed. Together they both moaned, as Stan instantly regretted his offering to get up early with his son. Now the excuses would begin.

"It's a bit early," Stan muttered, refusing to open his eyes. Billy shook him by the shoulder. He had seen the routine before, knowing it would take some effort for them to move. It would be worth it in the end, it always was. For him.

"Snowman, snowman, snowman," Billy shouted.

"We have to have breakfast first," Stan said, the first line of defense in his excuses for the day. Billy jumped off the bed, ran back to his room, grabbed a cereal bar off the drawers, opened it and ran back while eating. He jumped back on the bed, continued to jump up and down, all the while eating.

"There, done, time to get up," he said, still chewing. Nancy turned over, smiling to herself, glad she wasn't part of it, but still admiring her son's ingenuity.

Stan groaned. Time for part two. "Did you tidy your bedroom up?" he asked, still refusing to open his eyes.

Billy shrugged. He was used to having to work to get his mum and dad up for winter days, but it was never easy, or fun.

"You didn't tell me to," Billy replied.

"Well, you go do that, and while you're doing it, I'll get up and dressed," Stan offered.

Billy stood straight up on the bed. "OK great, I'll go do it quickly," he said, running straight out. The moment he cleared the door Stan turned over, stretched out and sighed, ready for another hour or two of sleep.

Billy ran into his room, began grabbing things off the floor and shoving it quickly into drawers.

"Don't forget under the bed, clean that bed now," his father said, just for good measure.

Arthur had slowly begun to become aware that something was going on, slowly because he had slept so well, and was comfortable being wrapped up in several old socks and a large towel. Comics and books had piled up under the bed, providing him with just the right amount of safety from being seen, so he could relax all the more for it. Gently he lifted his head, peering over the pile to watch Billy go about his work.

Suddenly Billy made a grab at something near to him under the corner of his bed. Arthur's eyes lit up, as for the first time it seemed he might have a problem. He stared at the boy hastily grabbing at things, shoving them in drawers and tubs. He pulled a pair of pajama bottoms from the corner, before running out with them, to the bathroom, dropping them in the wash basket and back again. It was all too fast for Arthur to react, he simply had no choice but to watch and wait.

"Spiders, noooo," Billy shouted, jumping up and running. Once again he ran out, and returned before Arthur could move. Billy had picked up a long sweeping brush, ready to fend off an attack should it come from the hordes of tiny spiders that only existed in his mind.

Billy poked the brush hard under the bed, until he hit something soft. He imagined it was the hiding place of whatever hid under his bed at night, whether it was the bogey man or a spider named Jack, but whatever it was would have to go find somewhere else. The brush head caught Arthur square on the nose, making him jump. Any moment and it would be over, here comes the running, chasing and shouting!

The brush withdrew, right back, as Arthur watched, ready to sprint out. Billy took in a deep breath, held onto it tight, and dropped the brush, standing quickly up, bouncing around.

"Toilet, toilet, toilet," he muttered under his breath while holding his groin. Being in a mood for sudden gestures he quickly ran out, into the bathroom and slammed the door. It was all systems go as Arthur found his opening. He shuffled quickly out, crawling past the rubbish, plates, and books, before scrambling out to the landing. He looked around, wasting no time in heading for the stairs. He was in such a hurry he never even bothered to look back. If he had he would have seen Billy rushing back out of the bathroom, back into his room.

Arthur fled down the stairs, rushing headlong without a thought as to where he might go. Almost as if acting on instinct he headed straight into the kitchen, his mind focused on escaping, but his stomach focused on food, *now*.

Billy walked back into his room, satisfied that he could get through the next ten minutes without another break. He became a whirlwind, grabbing clothes, books, toys, comics, anything and everything and shoving it into anywhere that would fit. He sat down, took hold of the sweeping brush and pushed it right under the bed, sliding it sideways before pulling out everything underneath. As he pulled, an old t-shirt came out, one he had been hunting for ages, a Spiderman shirt, worn but one he loved. Again he pulled, as it resisted his efforts, one last pull, until out popped what was left of the turkey, well nibbled, almost nothing but bones.

What he was seeing shocked him, as much for the sight of seeing something so strange under his bed, but the thought of it soon changed when he realized just what it was, not just a well-eaten turkey, but the one missing from the fridge.

"How, how did that..." Billy began to say, almost too shocked for words. Then another thought hit him- what if someone walked in now, and saw him with a near completely eaten turkey? Panic set in, as he began to imagine what would happen when everyone thought he had eaten it, even though he hadn't.

Without thinking he grabbed at it, immediately regretting its greasiness, lifting it up as best he could, and stood up. It was a sight to see, him stood there in pajamas, surrounded by a bigger mess in his bedroom than when he had begun, holding a turkey that had somehow escaped from the fridge. He was totally at a loss.

He listened a moment, decided no one was up yet, figuring the best course of action was to avoid blame. He crept out of his bedroom door, onto the landing. His parents' door was mostly closed, and beyond his sister's door half open. As much as she liked her privacy, she was known to be afraid of the dark and liked an escape route, something he often enjoyed teasing her over.

Billy crept along the landing, looking like a cartoon burglar, seeking to tiptoe their way out of danger. He passed Mum and Dad's room, quietly as ever, until he stood outside Abigail's room. He stood on the spot, leaning into her room slowly. He figured any moment she might spot him and begin screaming. What she would make of him being there holding a mess of turkey bones he didn't know, but it wouldn't be good. Thankfully she was asleep, so fast asleep that she had fallen half off her bed, wrapped in her quilt, looking as if she might drop completely off any moment. It would be a fun sight to see, but given his predicament, he decided against it.

Creeping, tiptoeing, Billy edged into the bedroom. It was all pink and light, flowers and bright colors, with cushions dotted around and her walls covered in posters of boy bands. As horrible as he thought it was, for now he had a mission to accomplish. He walked halfway, then stopped, looked at her, listened, waited, and carried on a bit further. Abigail was snoring, something he had often accused her of, to his amusement. He struggled not to laugh about it, as her mouth wobbled when she breathed out. If only he could say something, but not today.

Billy dropped gently to the carpet, turkey in hands, onto his elbows, cradling it like a newborn baby. He pushed it under the bed, the nice clean space so much unlike his own, into the darkness beyond. There it sat, like a prize bird on display. Job done he pulled out, stood quickly up, checked once more to see she was still asleep, and once again crept out.

As he edged out of the Abigail's room he turned around, ready to head back to his own room. His head bumped into something large but soft, an immovable object heading in the same direction as he. He looked up to see his dad looking down at him. His mind lit up to what was coming.

"Morning Billy, have you tidied your room up yet?" Stan asked him. The expression on his face, at least for the moment, suggested he was none the wiser to what was going on.

"Er, yes, Dad, just..."

"Just what?"

"Er..."

"Why were you in Abigail's room?"

The game was up, he was rumbled, it was all over. As he thought about all the implications of what the discovery would do to him, Billy caught sight of the snow outside from the window. Fireworks lit up in his mind, tragedy.

"I, I, I, er, I thought I smelled something funny," he suddenly said, wiping his hands on the back of his pajamas. It was a hopeful effort at an excuse, and not one anyone would ever fall for.

"Really, what kind of smell, not gas?" Stan asked, looking worried all of a sudden.

"No," Billy replied all too excitedly, equally as amazed that anyone would buy it; surely not.

Stan sniffed the air, unable to smell anything that could be a problem. "Sorry, nothing there."

The response made Billy think, if he couldn't smell anything, then he might once again ask him why he was in Abigail's room. That would be a problem.

"Can I go outside to play now, Dad?" Billy asked, offering his best smile.

"Sure," Stan replied succinctly.

"Yes," Billy shouted, jumping for joy.

"Is your room tidy?" Stan asked before Billy could run away.

Billy stopped in his tracks and looked at his dad. "Nearly, I'll finish it now," he said.

"Sure, but what smell?" Stan asked, not giving in at all. Billy frowned, knowing he was beaten.

A spark of inspiration hit him, a once in a lifetime thought that would change everything.

"I'm not sure what it was, it was coming from Abigail's room, I went in to see what it was. I think it was coming from around her bed," Billy said, rolling the dice, one last shot at being in the clear. In his mind it was probably Abigail who had eaten the thing and left it under his bed anyway, so she deserved it.

"Oh," Stan said, not believing it for one moment. Without saying anything else, he knocked gently on Abigail's door, noticed it was near open and walked in. Billy followed, wondering how long he could walk the tightrope of his one-man act, without falling off.

Once again Stan sniffed the air, looking every bit the hound looking for his next meal. He pulled a face and looked at Billy. "You know, I can smell it too, smells a bit meaty."

Billy looked shocked, before realizing he shouldn't give anything away. He looked like a clown, making faces as he went through a range of emotions.

"Abigail," Stan shouted, making her snap too. The moment she woke, she began to rub her neck, regretting having slept so soundly.

"What?" she asked grumpily.

"What's that smell?" Stan asked again, suddenly realizing it was an awkward question.

"What's that under your bed?" Billy shouted before anyone else could intervene. He was pointing directly at the bed.

"What's what?" Abigail asked, now sitting up and rubbing her eyes.

Stan looked at Billy, followed his accusing finger, to Abigail, then down, underneath the bed. He crouched over, trying to see in the darkness. He knew very well how clean Abigail liked to keep things, expecting to find nothing.

"Why are you both in my room? Get out please," Abigail said, finally waking up to what was going on. As she spoke Nancy walked in, wondering what all the fuss was about.

"No way, I don't believe it," Stan said. Abigail looked at him annoyed, ready to explode at the sudden invasion of her room. Billy watched on, struggling not to smirk at his success, his game plan had worked.

Stan dropped to one knee, leaned under the bed, and pulled out the remnants of the turkey, standing up with it in his hands. "Abigail, surely not," he asked, looking directly at her.

Abigail looked completely shocked, her mood swinging from anger to upset and more. She didn't know whether to scream or cry.

"Oh my, what have you been up to?" Nancy asked.

"Yeah Abigail, what have you been up to?" Billy demanded, pleased that he was on the winning side for once.

"That's ridiculous, Billy you put that there," Abigail shouted back.

"No, I didn't. Mum, tell her!" Billy shouted.

"Enough, Billy, go finish your room and get dressed, you can go out to play when that's done," Stan insisted, clearly in no mood to argue. Billy ran out, jumping as he did, pleased that finally he could do what he wanted. All thoughts of turkey were gone.

Nancy looked at Stan, totally confused. Abigail looked up at Stan and Nancy, ready to react if anyone said the wrong thing.

Stan looked at Nancy, then Abigail, a calm, measured look on his face, perfectly at ease with what was to come.

"Abigail, I know you like turkey, but not that much," he said, chuckling to himself.

"Stan," Nancy said firmly.

"Dad, I..." Abigail began.

"Yes, I am well aware that it wasn't you who ate the turkey, and I am well aware it wasn't you that put this under your own bed," he said, finally lowering the temperature of the room. He looked at them both, smiling pleasantly, pleased that he had handled it so well.

"So how come Billy is allowed to go out?" Abigail demanded.

"Calm yourself, no point in getting all worked up over it. I'll talk it over with him later, but for now I shall go dispose of what's left of our dinner."

Nancy glared at him as he left, more annoyed that he had found it funny. As he walked out she looked at Abigail, who had no intention of being anyone's scapegoat.

Morning had begun, and the trials were only just beginning.

As all the fuss was going on upstairs, Arthur had just sat, in the downstairs hall, looking up, wondering if it was time to leave. There was nothing to eat in the kitchen, save for some scraps on the floor. He had slept so well, felt refreshed, and thought how a nice long walk might feel. Instinctively he welcomed it, but still, memories of the open road left him thinking about the long cold days, and time without food. Time for leaving hadn't come around yet.

Running and jumping upstairs brought his attention back to the now, as footsteps on the stairs followed. He looked at the kitchen, too open, the games room, possibly around the teddies, or the lounge, not great options, but he would have to choose. Bright lights filtered in from the lounge with the door wide open, as if it were calling to him. Without another thought, he trotted over to the door, walked in and looked around. There were two large sofas, and a large chair, all plush and soft, very much welcoming, especially if he wanted to be spotted and have his bottom kicked. His mind showed him images of himself being laid upside down on the chair, legs in the air, chops wide open, snoring for all the world to hear. His reality would be much different, involving kicks to the bottom and angry faces, he knew that much from experience.

"I'll go put this in the bin," Stan said, walking down the next flight of stairs. Nancy nodded to him, heading on to the kitchen.

Arthur walked to the middle of the lounge, looked around, and leaped towards the sofa, at first intending to jump on it, to look out of the huge window. At the last minute, he changed direction, heading for the gap behind, dark and welcoming. It was tight, but doable. He shoved in head first, then pulling himself, squeezed his body in, pushing so hard the sofa shifted away from the wall. He dragged himself along, until he was all the way in. It was so tight there was no way to turn, and no going back. No matter, for now he could just lay and wait, time to see what happened.

Abigail came tumbling down the stairs, her hair looking as if it had been the victim of a hurricane, her face a picture of tiredness.

"What do you want for breakfast?" Nancy called as she spotted her go into the lounge.

"Turkey!" Billy shouted as he came running down. He laughed loudly as he continued down to the back door, ready for wellington boots and out.

"Billy!" Abigail shouted.

"Billy, get your coat on, and your gloves, and your wellington boots," Nancy shouted to him.

"I'm full, Mum, Abigail gave me some of her turkey," Billy called back, laughing even more. Nancy giggled before putting her hand over her mouth, not wanting to make things worse by seeming to enjoy it. There was still the matter of the wrongly eaten turkey after all.

Abigail walked quickly into the lounge, flopping face-first onto the sofa, unaware that she was inches away from a dog she had never met. The sofa shifted closer to the wall, squashing Arthur, making him wince. Any more and he would have to do something.

Stan walked in, took one look at Abigail and turned to walk out.

"My life is over," Abigail said before he could leave. Caught at the last moment.

"Oh yes dear, never mind," he said, once again trying to leave.

"Thanks for the sympathy, Dad."

"It's fine, I said that," Stan insisted.

"My brother is a turkey eating monster."

Stan thought of a range of things to say to brighten the mood, but settled on quietly walking out without saying a thing.

"Mum, I'm cold," Billy said, appearing at the kitchen door, shivering. He was wearing wellington boots but no coat or gloves.

"Billy!" Nancy said quickly. She rushed over to him, hugging him closer to herself. His hands and face were ice cold, his lips blue. Still, he had the spark of fun in his eyes, she could see how happy he was.

"Let's get some porridge with hot milk, that will warm you up," Nancy offered. Billy smiled back at her, nodding.

"I want bacon," Stan said, walking in, slippers flopping on the hard floor.

"I want turkey," Abigail said as she walked in. Everyone laughed.

For now, it was done, dealt with, and wouldn't be brought up again. Such was the understanding they all shared, a bond of love, and affection from which some things didn't need an explanation.

Together they sat around the kitchen table, enjoying a moment together, sharing the warmth and comfort of a good home.

Arthur used the moment, struggling like a bull trying to throw its rider. First he pulled, then pushed, then shook, tried to turn and ended up upside down. Finally he simply went for it, doing everything at once, before pushing against the sofa back with all his might. The sofa gave in, losing its battle against him, moving away so that he was free. He walked away, satisfied he had won, back out into the hall, back up the stairs. It had been a difficult start to the morning, and as hungry as he was, for now another few hours of sleep were welcome.

As he walked up the stairs he could hear the laughter and fun coming from the kitchen. It was something unusual for him, and something that he would love to be a part of. If only.

CHAPTER SEVENTEEN

Sleep wrapped itself around Arthur like a cozy blanket. It smothered and protected him, offering only his dreams for company.

At first it was an easy, fine sleep, memories of feeling happy and safe, what little there were of them. Then his mind pulled him away, onto things he had forgotten.

She was there, the lady, so quiet now, no longer moving. Her hair was gray. Memories of her now faded, her eyes closed, no more energy for walks. Arthur laid at her feet, feeling the coldness of the air around them, and of her, as he shivered from time to time, with the effect of it, and his own feelings.

The thoughts moved on, as feeling became stronger. Arthur whimpered in his sleep, loud enough to be known, but no one in the house noticed.

Now, there was the man again, walking in, looking surprised, not happy. Was he unhappy with Arthur? What was wrong? He came and knelt beside her, looking urgently, taking her hand. There seemed to be no happiness in the memory, only sadness and worry. The man stayed for a few minutes, his head down, not noticing Arthur. He made a noise, causing Arthur to jump, to move quickly away. The man began to speak on a telephone, saying things, sounding worse the more he spoke.

Arthur moved quickly away, fearful he had done something wrong. The man stood up, quickly going to the front door, opening it wide, looking out before returning to the woman again. He would not leave her alone again.

Then silence, except for the man sitting on the floor beside her, unable to raise his head.

It was enough for Arthur to understand. The door was open, he must leave, to go and be away from the only home he had ever known, to leave the woman be, for fear that he should be the cause of so much sorrow. Arthur ran out, into the cold air, the bright skies, for the first time in his life alone, running away, off down the streets. Where he headed he had no idea, all that he knew was to forget about his home, because he was no longer wanted.

Off he went, and never went back.

CHAPTER EIGHTEEN

Billy felt happy. It had begun to snow again, and his father had promised to take him to a hilltop later for some sledding. It was the weekend, and he had nothing else to do except have fun. Even Abigail had smiled at him, albeit briefly. The food had been just right, and as much as he wanted to go outside again, for the moment all he wanted to do was sit and play.

"Billy, make sure to clean your teeth please," Nancy said, just as he was about the leave the kitchen.

"OK Mum, I'll do it when Abigail has her monthly bath," he replied, immediately regretting it. Given how good things had been, he didn't want to spoil it, but being so young was too proud to say so to her. It didn't matter, she simply shrugged it off and walked away. He was thankful for it, but would never tell her so.

Stan stood up, wiped toast crumbs from his pajamas and smiled to himself. He too was glad at things, a full belly and warm from the toasty central heating. His cheeks glowed, reminding him of a time when he was young, sitting next to an open fire near his mother, heavy snow outside, just enjoying the peaceful nature of it all. There was an old black and white television on, a western, which he had never particularly enjoyed, but it didn't matter, because for those few moments it was nice to get warm, and be with her. Now he had his family, and they too could share something similar.

"Don't forget to clean your teeth," Billy shouted to his father as he walked away. Stan and Nancy looked at each other, laughing quietly. They had a precocious son, but they wouldn't change him for the world.

As Billy approached the stairs they suddenly became a challenge, as if he were to climb Everest. He leaned down a little, girded himself, before lunging at them, bounding up the stairs. One, then two at a time he went up, running around, onto the landing area, off to his room. He burst in, remembered he needed to clean his teeth, but deciding playing with toys was higher on his order of importance. He quickly sat down, grabbed a racing car and dropped into his own particular world of imagination.

"I'm going in the shower, then we'll get dressed and pop out, ok?" Stan called, walking past Billy's room. Billy barely noticed him, so lost in his own world of fun.

A shrill noise finally interrupted his fun, something so unusual it made no sense to his mind. Billy listened a moment more, then continued playing. It was nothing, and besides, shortly he would be going out, and for that he couldn't wait.

Another noise stopped him, this time like a whimper. It sounded like a puppy, playing. He thought perhaps his parents had gone and got them a puppy, something they had been nagging about for months, but unlikely. As if his mother would allow a dog in her perfectly tidy home.

A sudden loud yelp made Billy jump up. It was loud enough for him to be sure it was real. He looked around, across to his drawers, to all the corners of his room, nothing. Just as his eyes focused on the messed up bed covers, another louder yelp came, making Billy run quickly for the door.

"Muuuum!" he shouted, stepping away from his bedroom, not for a moment taking his eyes off of the door.

Nobody answered, so used were they to his calls, so often about nothing more than wanting a drink or something to eat. He was the typical boy who cried wolf, that needed something so quickly, urgently, seriously, and yet never really needed it at all.

"MUUUUUUUUUM," Billy shouted as loud as he could, at the very top of his croaky voice.

Nancy came running up the stairs. As much as he could be annoying, he never called in such a manner. She knew it must matter. At least, this time it had better matter.

She saw him standing on the landing, looking at his door, all wide-eyed and unsure of himself. It was very different of him. Rushing over, she took his hand, looking at him, concerned at his fright.

Abigail came rushing out, saw the two of them, and wondered if perhaps the concern might be that he needed a drink, or food, and a good excuse to get them. It didn't take long to realize she was wrong about him this time.

"Stan," Nancy called. He had done as he had said, gone in the shower, singing to himself at the top of his voice. He was having far too much of a good time to hear them.

Nancy leaned over, pushing open the door to the bedroom. It swung wide, making the bedroom clear to see for all of them. Other than a messy bedroom, with clothes all over and toys everywhere, they couldn't see anything out of order.

"Billy, you are hopeless," Abigail shouted, angry that he had misled them again.

"No, seriously, there was something in there making a noise," Billy pleaded. He looked up at his mother, showing he meant it. She couldn't see anything in the room, but she knew when he was being honest.

Nancy knew there was no alternative, as she turned to the bathroom door. She hammered on it with her fist, only for Stan to sing even louder.

"You know I can see where you get it from now, Billy," Nancy said, shrugging. She didn't fancy going into the room by herself. Without Stan for backup, and with her children looking ever more frightened, she had no choice. It would fall to her to find out what was going on.

"Abigail, go into my room, look in the tall cupboard and get me the sweeping brush." Nancy declared, more of an order than a request. Abigail didn't argue, thankful she wasn't the one to deal with it. A few seconds later she returned with a bright blue, plastic sweeping brush. She handed it to her mother, before stepping away again, making sure she wasn't going to be backup.

Reluctantly, Nancy took the brush and stepped forward into the room. Abigail moved closer to Billy, putting her arm around him. As creepy as he thought it was, he too was glad he wasn't going in.

The noises had stopped, with no further sounds coming from the room, but Nancy would take no chances. She edged in, brush at the fore, ready for action, hopeful that it would turn out to be nothing. She had decided if it was nothing, she wouldn't chastise Billy, accepting he had a vivid imagination.

Slowly she leaned over, looking under the bed, until clear as day she could see two bright eyes, gleaming in the light, staring back at her. Her first thought was to simply run out, slam the door and leave it to the man. As enticing as the idea sounded, she refused to accept that she couldn't deal with it, unless it turned out to be a tiger or something, in which case they would all leave the house and never return.

Nancy pushed the brush under the bed, entirely uncertain of what to do. She loathed the idea of using a brush in such a manner, but it was under her son's bed and nothing that could be a stranger could be allowed to go near her children. Needs must.

The brush poked under the edge, making the eyes move. They turned and moved, pulling back and away.

"No," Nancy shouted loudly, rushing back away, as a paw swiped out from under the bed at the brush. She ran out of the room, grabbing the children, as the eyes under the bed began to edge out.

The three of them stood watching, wondering whether to run or hide, or just scream all at once. The eyes moved, blinked, then moved again closer. They all watched, frozen to the spot, as a head peered out from under the bed, delicately, so slow that it seemed it was all in slow motion.

Now the eyes met theirs, as the little brown doggy pulled himself free from the bed, his tail hanging low beneath his body, his ears down, his eyes pleading for mercy, to be left alone... please.

"It's a dog," Abigail said, the most obvious statement any of them could make.

"You don't say," Billy replied, unable to stop himself from having a dig at his sister, even when something so odd was happening.

"Did you do this? Did you sneak a dog under your bed?" Abigail replied, enjoying her own dig at him.

Nancy looked at him, her face a picture of concern.

"Why would I sneak a dog in here, and then call you to tell you about it?" Billy asked. Nancy looked at him, surprised with his unusual clarity.

The little dog sat, knowing he was surrounded, wondering when the screaming and shouting might begin.

It was a stalemate, the three people looking at him, wondering what to do, the little dog looking at them, wondering what they were going to do, and more importantly, what he was going to do.

Everybody jumped as the bathroom door opened wide. Stan peered out, stood in his dressing gown, face and head covered by a towel as he rubbed his hair dry.

"Well, that was nice," he said, before realizing they were all stood outside his door.

"Wait, what are you all doing stood there?" Stan asked, looking at them in turn. The three looked at him, before slowly turning their attention to what the center of attention was. All eyes focused on the timid little dog in Billy's bedroom, sat quietly, looking at them, more afraid than he had ever been in his entire life.

“A dog,” Stan said loudly. Nancy wondered if such obvious statement ran in the family. Everyone took in a deep breath, before breathing out a deep sigh.

“It seems to have been hiding under Billy’s bed. Billy called us about it, so clearly he had no idea it was under there,” Nancy said.

“Wow, that’s crazy,” Stan replied.

Arthur just looked at them, knowing the game was up. He had seen the snow outside, and wasn’t looking forward at all to being back on the streets. It was life, it was as it was, and nothing was going to change it. It was the story of who he was, and now he was a street dog, foraging for food wherever he could get it, and likely destined to never again know what it was to be loved in quite the same way that he had before with the wonderful lady, who had only ever shown him and others kindness and love no matter what, no questions asked.

Stan gently moved around the family, ready to protect them if need be. He could talk to the little dog, make sure it wasn’t dangerous, and perhaps lock it in until someone could be called for assistance, to take him away, wherever that might be.

Stan leaned over, looked at him, and waited. Abigail, Billy, and Nancy all watched, wondering if something bad was going to happen.

“*Arthur*?” Stan said quietly. His words were almost a whisper, barely able to give life to them.

Arthur’s ears pricked up at hearing his name. He knew it well, but it had been so long since anyone had used it with him. His eyes glittered in the light again, offering a deeply held kindness that had been hidden for too long.

Stan leaned down, before kneeling, right in front of him.

“It can’t be, can it?” Stan muttered under his breath.

“Be careful, Dad, you don’t know,” Abigail began.

Before she could say anything more, Stan lifted out his hands, taking a gentle hold of the dog around his ears and neck. He looked around at him, studying him, before looking into his eyes.

“It is you, Arthur,” he said.

"How could you possibly know this dog?"

"You don't recognize him? I know it's been years, he looks so different, but it is, it's him, it's your Gran's dog, Arthur. He ran away when..." Stan couldn't finish his sentence.

Everyone fell silent, looking, as Stan took a hold of the dog, hugging him. Now Arthur knew, he could tell, this was the man, the one who shouted, had been so upset, made him run away. As the man hugged him tightly, he knew how wrong he had been to leave, how much he was still needed. Arthur closed his eyes, enjoying the moment, no longer thinking of the future, or the past, but only of now.

Finally, Stan turned to look at his family, tears in his eyes. "He's home now, he's back home with us, forever," he said. Nobody would disagree with him, least of all Billy.

"Yes! We've got a dog," he shouted happily, as he and Abigail rushed to share their affection.

"Well," Nancy said firmly. All eyes turned to her, including Arthur's. "he's not going to stay here."

The mood instantly dropped, but before the pleading could begin, she spoke again. "He's not going to stay here until he's had a bath," she said, smiling.

Everyone laughed, all hands hugging their new dog. Arthur had found a new home, one that was waiting for him all along.

THE END

Did you enjoy this book?

If you did, please consider leaving a review on the Amazon website. Good reviews encourage writers to write as well as helping to promote our creative works to others.

Whether it is a few words or a few sentences, if you could spend a few moments of your time with this it would be much appreciated.

Out Now!

The Dog Under The Bed 2: Arthur On The Streets

Find out what happened to Arthur before he ended up under a little boy's bed. What he went through, and how life is for a lonely little dog on the streets, unwanted and unloved.

Out Now!

The Dog Under The Bed 3: What Happened Next

The loving conclusion to the series, as Arthur not only comes to terms with his new family, but finally confronts the past, ready for a loving future.

Filled with laughter, tears and joy, What Happened Next show us just why we love dogs so much.

Made in the USA
Coppell, TX
09 June 2020